First Born of the Moon

And Other Stories

Michael P. Andre

Copyright © 2015 Michael P. Andre
All rights reserved.
ISBN-13 978-0-9937384-1-8 (Paperback)
ISBN 978-0-9937384-0-1 (e-book

DEDICATIONS

I dedicate this to my wife and family.

ACKNOWLEDGEMENTS

I thank Saima, Denis, and my sister, Joanne for their help in editing most of the stories in this book.

TABLE OF CONTENTS

INTRODUCTION

This compilation is the result of many years of effort or lack thereof. You will see that ideas for stories came sporadically, beginning when I was around twelve years old, through my teenage years, and beyond.

Now, when I say writing, I mean writing by hand, as our family did not have a typewriter. Later in my teens, my family acquired a typewriter and I switched to that mode of writing.

In my late teens, I joined my high school's literary club. There, students wrote poems and stories and read them aloud to the other members for critiquing. At the end of the year, we put together a small booklet of our efforts.

My writing lacked refinement at that time; one reason being that it was much more difficult to edit stories. I had to rewrite or retype the whole page if there were any substantial changes to the text required – nothing like now with cutting and pasting on a computer.

Then, life took hold. University diverted me from my writing. I became involved in community volunteer work and held two jobs. Earning a living and advancing in my career was my focus. I got married and had children, which further occupied my time.

Around 1995, I dusted off what I had written and started to key it into the computer. In this way, I got almost all my poems transcribed, as well as two or three stories at an early stage of completion and the beginnings of one or two books.

I stopped writing again until around 2005 when I edited some of the stories I had written. Things quieted again until late in 2009, when I began to realise that, if I did not get back to writing soon, I would never publish my stories I had entered a new decade of life perhaps, when many people become more aware of their mortality. I put aside my quiet time of reading or playing computer games to do my life's other dream: to write – maybe too late but certainly better than never.

Most of my stories are science fiction but some would fit into other genres. I became enamoured with science fiction at an early age. One book I remember, which may be the first, or certainly one of the first, books I read, was *Marooned on Mars* by Lester Del Ray. I was hooked. Some other great authors also influenced me such as Isaac Asimov, Arthur C. Clark, Robert A. Heinlein, H. G. Wells, and others. I was fascinated by the television series *The Twilight Zone* and later *Star Trek*. You will likely see some of those influences in my work.

When I got more serious with writing, I found it required a lot of work and patience. What I find frustrating is when I have finished a review, I find more errors in a subsequent edit. I have edited some of these stories maybe twenty times or more. When I passed them on to friends to read, they would have other recommendations for change. I guess writing is almost like having a baby: there is a lot of pain and pushing but it sure is wonderful when it ends.

What I find wonderful about writing is when I am finally satisfied with the result but also this – and I will quote from Beatrix Potter because this says it all: "There is something delicious about writing the first words of a story. You never quite know where they'll take you".

This is true. When I have an idea for a story, it is often mostly formed in my mind. I start to write then my fingers tell the story and fill in all the beautiful details. However, I do not think it applies just to the first words but even to the last, as sometimes those are the most surprising.

I hope you enjoy reading these stories as much as I have enjoyed writing them.

FIRST BORN OF THE MOON

This story was 'born' in the fall of 2009. I just woke up one morning with a story in my head. I let my fingers do the rest. It is about a young woman who is planning for many changes to her life, with getting married and moving to Earth.

She stared out of the portal into the grey brightness. She would soon see this no more. She would no longer peer at the familiar shadows and the dust that had rested undisturbed for billions of years. She gazed at humankind's footsteps that would now rest in the dust for all eternity. The building she was in would remain here like a monument to the ingenuity, resourcefulness, and perseverance of the top of Earth's living food chain. Humans evolved through the long chain of chemical stews from the early tides of ancient Earth and now rested in a new stew that could not maintain the tiny foothold in space they had so dearly prized. They were slinking away from their greatest pride and shrivelling from their most fundamental desire: to spread their seed across the Earth and to continue from there into the emptiness of space, the new wild frontier.

A tear trickled from her eye. This was her home, the only home she knew. She raised her gaze to the great coloured ball lighting up the sky. Her mother and father had often told her how beautiful Earth was and constantly referred to it as home. Their love of it had developed in her a powerful attraction to that glowing ball and home to humanity. She had a longing to walk someday on its surface to visit the many relatives she had seen in pictures and talked with on the computer. Her mother and father had returned to Earth several years ago but she had decided to remain behind.

She was born on the Moon two years after the new settlers arrived. She was the first born of the Moon and her mother named her Luna. Future children would tease her with "Luna, Luna of the Moona" but when she found out what her name meant, she felt proud, and would return, "And you're not".

Being the firstborn had its advantages. She was fawned over by everyone on the base but that created a problem when another couple had a baby a little over two years later. She was no longer number one and she resented it and acted out her frustration for almost a year until she learned to accept it. As other babies arrived on the scene, she realised she could still be number one, as she was the oldest, and took the smaller ones under her wing to create a mini-community on the base with her in charge, and she loved it. What the adults did, she recreated in miniature with her charges. The Moon had become her little empire. The other children did not stay long, however, as their parents left after their five-year term or one extended term.

Her father was the chief engineer of the base and kept renewing his terms, so there she remained. By eight, she considered herself its owner and began scratching her initial on the lower edges of the doorframes. As she grew older, she learned the Colonel was the commander of the base but to her, the engineers were more important. They were the ones to whom everyone went to sort out problems, and often make decisions. People's lives were in their hands. That was what she wanted as her career.

When she completed her schooling, she applied to and was accepted at, an engineering school on Earth. She took her classes by correspondence and by videoconference but the university insisted she complete her last two years in class. She was thrilled to go and visit that beautiful globe in the sky. She wanted to confirm all the beautiful things her parents had told her about it. Instead, she lived through the worst years of her life. The only things she enjoyed were the colours of the plants, animals, and advertising signs, as well as meeting some of her relatives. Her special joy came with her graduation, cum laud.

For almost two years, she had found Earth stifling hot or unbearably cold. She had to endure its stenches, odours, and perfumes. The noises of its rushing masses of people and machines overwhelmed her. She constantly suffered from its myriad diseases and allergic reactions to its endless varieties of pollen and spores. Although her doctor had given her countless serum injections, she was sick for most of her stay. In her early days on the planet, Earth's crushing gravity had forced her into a wheelchair. She never walked normally on its surface. Oddly, Earth looked better from afar, from the Moon's portal. That beautiful glow she viewed each day of her life had been a nightmare. Earth was where she was going now, to stay, to make her new life with her betrothed, Rick.

Now, Earth's officials had given her the honour of being one of the last persons to leave the Moon, firstly because of her birth but also because she was now its chief engineer after the previous chief left to go back to Earth two years ago. She was there to shut down Moon Base 1. They had not completed Moon Base 2.

This was a sad day for her. She was leaving the moon and overwhelmed with her trip back to Earth, her wedding, and finding a home. These were all normal activities for a couple in love and looking forward to spending their lives together. She loved children and looked forward to that more than anything else. Even though she was busy in her role as an engineer, she had spent many hours each week volunteering to look after the children of the base, either in the school or as part of daycare services.

She looked down at her watch and was a little shocked to find how much time had passed. She had to get to the greenhouse and then the central control unit to start the process of shutting down all the functions on the base. Rick, an engineer himself, was in the power centre shutting down the nuclear power unit. The base would soon run on battery and solar panels for the final shutdown phase.

Rick had been on the base for six years now. For the first four, they had not noticed each other. They were both dedicated to their jobs and the last thing on their minds was romance. He was fascinated with life and work on the Moon and much too busy learning how everything functioned.

One day, they were discussing a project and she was explaining how the computer system linked to the nuclear power control system. She was working at a table covered with sheets of schematics when she turned her head and noticed he was no longer looking at the schematics.

Over the next two years, their romance blossomed outside of working hours. They had planned a wedding on the Moon when they heard that Moon Base was closing. Everyone on the base knew they had no choice but to leave, as the base was not sustainable without constant support from Earth. The work involved in the shutdown was intense and took almost all their time. There was not just the physical shutdown of the base but there were all the arrangements to shuttle everyone off the base and into the spaceships back to Earth. All senior personnel on the base were involved in the process in one way or another. Rick and Luna had decided it would be better to wed on Earth. Her parents were now planning a huge wedding gala with every relative present to witness the event and help get the newlyweds established in their new home and life together.

She arrived at the greenhouse door and paused. She bent down to feel the little 'L' scratch by the door. She stepped inside. The room was now almost bare. Gone were the rows and rows of plants that had provided fruits and vegetables for the people on the base and purified the air. Gone were the limited number of flowers grown with no function other than to remind the occupants of Earth through their colours and scents. She had often picked some for her mother. Gone now was the imaginary jungle in which she had lived as a child and where she had played hide and seek with the other children.

She watched the two mechanical robots that had been her soldiers in the jungle and had gone with her on imaginary quests to other planets. She had given them names from the classic Star Wars movies she had watched repeatedly in her youth – R2D2 and C3PO – although they did not look anything like the originals in the movies. They had multiple arms with the tools necessary for their functions as gardeners: shovels, hoes, rakes, clippers, etc.

The two robots had almost completed their task. She helped them empty the last beds of plants and store the equipment in the storage room. After a quick inspection to ensure everything was complete, she guided the robots to their spot in that room. "Goodbye to each of you," she said, as she patted them each in turn. She hesitated a second, then shut them off, removed their batteries, and stored them in a special storage compartment. Her instructions to take such care to shut down the base properly seemed odd if Earthlings never intended to come back here.

She left the greenhouse and walked to the washroom, then stooped to feel the little mark beside its door. She entered the washroom and looked at herself in the mirror. She could see her resemblance to her parents, a father who had always been busy around the base but loved her dearly, and a mother who doted on her. With her parents gone from the base, Rick had taken that role. She smiled a bit. She had never felt attractive before but Rick had changed all that. She knew he loved her and she loved him back.

She left the washroom and moved on to the central control unit, which was in one wing of the base. It had a large double air-lock door on one outside wall to allow the entry of large equipment into the base. Three other rooms on the base had smaller double airlock exit doors, A, B, and C, which allowed entry to smaller articles, including people; exit A being the closest to the launch pad. For safety, the engineers ensured that, if a meteor hit room, no other room would lose air.

When she got to the access door of the control room, there too was her little mark but she did not bend down to touch it. Luna knew it was there. She punched in her entry code and the door opened. She entered, walked over to the control seat, and sat down. She pulled out her checklist. She was on the last page. She checked off the items dealing with the greenhouse and looked at the control panel. The nuclear pile was now offline. She could see Rick in the power control room through the monitor. He had stored the uranium rods, and drained and stored the fluids. He was now disconnecting some of the equipment and moving it into a storage area.

She smiled as she watched him work. It would not be long now before they would be suiting up for their walk to the shuttle that would take them to the ship to Earth and soon after that, their new life together. He also wanted a family.

Rick's last task was to disconnect most of the batteries and store them but first, she would cut the power to the entire base. All that would remain was basic power from the solar panels linked to a couple of batteries, which would supply sufficient power to provide basic lighting to the base and run the computer, the air pumps, and doors, as well as the heaters that would keep some items, like the batteries, at a temperature controlled enough so they would not be damaged by the extreme heat and cold fluctuations the base would be subjected to on the Moon.

Her last task would be to activate the program for the base computer to complete the shutdown process. A few minutes after they left, the program would start the pumps to suck the air out of the base into the storage cylinders. After that, it would turn out the lights and put itself to sleep. The base would be ready for reactivation if needed in the future.

As she sat watching Rick, she thought of Earth. She wondered what her life would be like when she got there. She had her dreams with Rick but her impressions of Earth were not good. Here it had been so remote and peaceful.

For decades, many countries had dreamed of venturing into space and establishing colonies there. This resulted in a push to establish a base on the moon, and then Mars. At the instigation of the United States of America and with the agreement and collaboration of the European Union, Russia, China, Japan, Australia, India, and several other major countries of the world, they spent trillions of dollars to achieve this dream.

Now, the nations of Earth were in turmoil. Having drained the planet of its oil and other resources, polluted its air and water, and now fallen into financial ruin, the Earth's nations could no longer support their dreams for space. Amid the Earth-wide riots and strife, the United States alone was desperately bringing home the colonists of Mars and the Moon using money it could no longer afford. The rioters had already assassinated one president and law and order broke down quickly.

Movement on her monitor startled Luna and she snapped out of her dream-like state. Rick was waving at her to catch her attention. Her face brightened instantly as she cheerfully waved back. He returned her smile. As Rick's work finished, he turned to leave the power centre.

She typed the final command into the computer, entered it, and turned off the screen. The plan now was to meet him at the door to the greenhouse and they would proceed to exit A to go to the washroom and suit up for their departure from the base. They would then walk to the lunar module to drive to the launch pad and leave the Moon forever.

She stood up to leave but hesitated for almost thirty seconds, then sat down again. She reactivated the monitor and switched its input to another camera. She saw Rick walking briskly up a corridor. She smiled and, with a tear in her eye, put her right hand up to her lips and touched the screen. Her hands went to the keyboard, hesitated again, then typed and entered a series of commands. Suddenly, a red light began to blink and a horn to blow. A loud hissing noise started, as the seal to the large exterior door in her compartment broke and the air of her room rushed out.

Rick heard the ruckus and began to race toward the sound. He passed the greenhouse where Luna was supposed to meet him and reached the control room door. He furiously started hammering on the door with his fists yelling "Luna, Luna, what are you doing? Open this door. Let me in."

The hissing slowly ended. The horn stopped blowing. The light stopped blinking. Rick stopped banging. There was an absolute penetrating silence. Then, Rick collapsed on the floor sobbing.

He looked at his watch through his tears, knowing he was now late for the rocket to Earth but they were waiting for him. He got up, wiped his eyes, and blew his nose. He turned and slowly made his way to exit A. When he reached the end of the corridor, he turned one last time and stared sadly at the control room door. He placed his right hand up to his lips and blew her a kiss. He loved her. He understood her. She was home.

NOMADS

I was riding the bus on the way to work one morning in February 2009 when this story appeared in a frosty bus window. Here, two children go for a hike only to find some articles that will tell them about their ancestral past.

Mohammed opened his eyes and smiled at the new day. He went to the tent window and peered out. It was a black, starry morning. The sun had not risen yet but the day's glow would soon begin removing the veil of blackness from the night. He would begin another day of chores but what he liked best was his opportunity to explore.

His family had never stayed long in one place; a few months here, and a few weeks there, as they had done for several generations. His father followed the work and his family followed him. Their last trip had taken them from the deserts of the west, into these lands where the soil could support some crops. However, times had been hard and the rains scarce. Even here, the work was not abundant and the dust of the sand and sparse soil would soon fill their nostrils with gritty mud.

His father would be calling him to their dawn prayers soon, so he hurried to get ready. He poked at his sister, Yasmin, to alert her to the impending call. She woke quickly, scrambled out of bed, and dressed. She reached for one last piece of her kit.

"Are we going out?" she asked in Arabic.

"Yes," Mohammed answered.

"I don't think I'll ever get used to wearing a burqa."

"Shush, someone may hear you. You'll accommodate in time. You know you're getting older and you must cover yourself."

"But I can't see well in it and it's so hot during the day."

Mohammed pretended not to hear her, took her hand, squeezed it, and said, "Come, let's go."

Their father pushed open the cloth door to their part of the tent and saw they were ready to join him. As Yasmin left the tent, she put on her burqa. The family placed their mats on the hardpacked soil and bent to pray.

When finished, Mohammed's mother and sister went to start breakfast. He and his father worked on the chores they had promised to do for the farmer who had hired them. God had blessed his father with great manual skills in the art of carpentry and the gift of carrying out general repairs. His mother was a gifted mender. All the farmer would be able to pay them for a couple of weeks of work were meals, two bags of flour and a couple of chickens but it was something to eat and sustain them. Three other farmers had chores for him. Mohammed would have a lot to do over the next few weeks but sometimes they would go weeks without getting work.

The family stopped for prayers at sunrise and returned to work. Before noon, they were all invited to wash, dine, and say prayers with the farmer. When they finished, the farmer pulled Mohammed's father aside, out of earshot of the family. His mother knew right away the men wanted privacy and decided to send the two children off to play.

"Peace be upon you," the farmer started.

"And to you be peace," Mohammed's father replied.

"I have news for you."

"Yes?"

"Remember Ahmed Sheik?"

"Yes."

"He had his farm confiscated."

"What?"

"Confiscated – he was not properly following his faith. He and his family have been sent away for religious training."

"Why are you telling me this?"

"Because you could get his farm if Allah is willing."

"I am not a farmer."

"But you could be. I know this place is not one of great abundance but even in a bad year one can raise some chickens and animals for eggs, milk, and meat. There is also some game occasionally, praise Allah. Settling down will provide a better home for your family. We have a little school here, as you know, and your son could get an education."

"We've always been wanderers. Settling down is not for us."

"You should not take too long acting on my advice. There is no one now who is interested in the land but in time, someone else will take it and you may not get another chance. You are a good man and true to your faith; you are most deserving."

"I will give it some thought. I have nothing to offer for the place."

"If you are interested, see our Imam. He is a good man and may be able to help you. He will need references from other Imams you have known in your travels. You should let him know if you are interested soon, so he may choose you over others."

Now, Mohammed's father had much to ponder. His wife later asked about his discussion with the farmer but he chose not to tell her. This was something he had the power to decide on his own.

During this discussion, Mohammed and Yasmin were off on one of their daily adventures before afternoon prayers. This was Mohammed's favourite part of the day.

Mohammed always started his series of treks in the direction of Mecca, as he always considered that direction as being the luckiest. When they got a kilometre away, Yasmin asked if she could take off her burqa.

He scanned the land around them, saying. "It looks okay; nobody's close by. Watch out though."

Yasmin pulled off her covering.

Mohammed had only about three and a half hours of free time and had walked briskly to cover as much ground as he could. So far, they had not seen anything of great interest. He was almost ready to turn back when they spotted something ahead of them. He decided to go just a little farther. Soon they reached the remains of an old wooden house that had partly collapsed in on itself. The wind, sand and dust had eroded the exposed boards until they were almost paper-thin.

"I wonder how old this is?" he asked quietly.

"Looks old," Yasmin responded.

They surveyed the area around the structure but thought it was too dangerous to go inside.

Suddenly, the sand gave way under one of Yasmin's feet and it became lodged in a hole in the ground. She stood helplessly unable to pull out her foot.

"What's this?" she cried out in pain.

Mohammed looked down and saw her foot had punctured a board hidden under the sand. He bent down to examine it, gingerly twisted her foot a little, and pulled it out. Yasmin sat down in the sand to nurse her sore foot while she watched her brother.

He had begun to examine the empty hole and to pull at the broken board. It snapped and he threw the plank off to the side. He brushed the sand away from the small hole he had created to find several other planks that formed a cover to a room under the ground. He pulled out several other boards. He could see stairs leading into the opening. He tested the first step and found it was strong enough to bear his weight. As he continued down the steps, one by one, he soon found himself at the bottom.

The light from above shone brightly into the interior. The little underground room was only about three metres deep and four metres square. The area seemed too large to store provisions but too small to be anything else but a shelter. What he saw inside seemed to confirm his suspicions.

There was a bench that could seat about four people. Along one wall was some shelving where he spotted some bottles and cans of something, probably preserves. Some of the cans looked as if they had leaked their contents onto the shelf and the floor below, although water that had seeped into the shelter from time to time had washed the leakage on the floor. The water had never been more than a few centimetres deep – another sign of the scarcity of water in this area. On another wall was a small shelf containing what looked like two books. His curiosity aroused, he reached out to the books and dusted the top of them off with his hands. He picked up each one in turn and examined their exteriors. He noticed that someone had hidden a folded piece of paper under the two books. It was now brittle with age. It was apparent these objects had been there a very long time.

He carefully opened each book. He was not familiar with the script, so he could not understand what they said. He returned the books to a different part of the shelf and picked up the paper. He gingerly unfolded a part of it but could not understand it either. It appeared to be a coloured drawing. He refolded the paper, although a few chips of paper fluttered to the ground.

He paused to decide what to do. He knew their leaders banned these things and may get him into trouble if he brought them home. On the other hand, they may be of interest to the Imam.

He could see by the angle of the light, he had better decide soon, or he would be very late for afternoon prayers. He called up to Yasmin.

"Yasmin, how is your foot?"

She peered over the edge of the hole. "It's better but still sore."

"Can you walk, okay?"

"I think so but I may not be able to walk fast. What's down there?"

"I found a few interesting things. I wonder if I should bring them home."

"Are they heavy?"

"Not really. It's getting late. It's going to be difficult to get home on time. We'll have to hurry."

He grabbed the three articles and left the shelter. Above the ground, he opened his little knapsack and the two of them had a drink of water. He placed the objects into the sack. It was a tight fit.

Mohammed set a very quick pace towards home. Although Yasmin found it hard to keep up with her sore ankle, she tried her best. Mohammed stopped twice for a brief rest and drink of water. As seasoned nomads, they adapted to life on the move. As they approached home,

Yasmin put her burqa back on in case the farmer was around.

Their parents were waiting for them and they were not pleased. They noticed Yasmin's limp, did a quick inspection of her foot, and led them quickly to prayer.

When prayers were complete, they listened to the story of their children's adventure. His father looked at his wife and gave her a little nod. She pulled Yasmin with her to start supper.

When they left, Mohammed pulled out his treasure to show his father, who examined it and told him they would have to take it to the Imam.

Mohammed placed the articles back into the sack.

They ate supper in silence. As soon as they finished, the father picked up the small sack and Mohammed followed him on the trek to the home of the local Imam.

They arrived and knocked on the door. After the cordialities, Mohammed's father stated his business and pulled out the articles. The Imam looked them over with interest then motioned for the father to have his son leave the room and close the door.

Mohammed sat quietly on the chair near the door. He could hear murmuring but could not make out what they were saying. After about sixty minutes, the door opened and the two men led Mohammed out of the house and into the backyard. In the centre of the yard was a large fire pit. The two men loaded the pit with kindling and wood and soon had a roaring blaze going.

The Imam turned toward the boy.

"It is a good thing you collected these things and brought them to me. These things are bad. They can lead people to sin. All books but the Holy Books are bad and we must burn them, so people may not be led astray, or be distracted with imaginary stories. Prayer and work keep people happy and in harmony.

"The fire is nice and hot now, so you may have the honour of throwing these things into it. May Allah reward you for your good act."

One by one, Mohammed took each object and threw it into the fire. He watched the blaze consume them. The three of them threw several more logs onto the pyre to ensure nothing would remain of the evil objects. When the fire finally started to die down into red-hot coals, the Imam thanked them again for their act. "Allah will shine his light upon you, Allah is the greatest."

The father and son returned home. It was now almost time for night prayers.

"Come, son, and sit with me."

Mohammed followed his father to a fallen tree not far from his family's tent and the farmer's house. They used it as a bench. They sat down and talked softly so the sound of their voices would not carry too far. Mohammed realised his father was about to tell him something very important.

"You are old enough now for me to tell you the story of our family. You must not say anything about this to anyone. My father passed this on to me from our ancestors and now I pass this on to you. Someday you may pass this on to your sons."

"Not even Mother and Yasmin?"

"No, not even them."

Mohammed waited in anticipation. He felt honoured to receive the gift of his father's words. He respected that these words were for him alone and he would not repeat them to anyone outside his family line.

"We were not always nomads. Our story begins before then, in the time of the troubles.

"Many years ago, our society was different from now. It was almost a magical world, with machines that flew in the sky and magical boxes that showed images that talked but it also was a troubled world with many wars and other machines that killed people. There were so many things available people wanted to get what everyone else had, and soon the world filled with all these things. There were so many religions nobody knew which one was the true religion and some people chose to believe in nothing. There were so many languages few people could understand each other. It was a time when people fought other lands, when tribe fought tribe, when people of one religion fought people of other religions, when people of one language fought those of another language when women fought their husbands, children rebelled against their fathers, and families were torn apart."

Mohammed gasped.

"Then, the troubles came. Some people of Allah, the Heroes, revolted against all this and gave their lives so the infidels could hear the word of Allah, which came down to us from His Great Prophet, Allah is the greatest. Many of the Heroes gave their lives but many more of the infidels lost theirs and they began to realise their plight was hopeless. They are tired of the wars and death. They had no stomach for it. The infidels began to realise the word of Allah must be the True Faith and many of them began to turn to Him. Soon the great armies of His Faithful covered the Earth and brought peace. They eliminated all diversions from peace and Allah. They eliminated all machines and even books other than the Koran because they were contaminants of the mind and soul.

"The Believers of Allah were favoured and received land to sustain them. When they destroyed their machines, the people in the large cities had nothing to live on and had to work the land and sea for sustenance. The large cities emptied and remain crumbling in that state. Many people resisted the spread of the True Faith for many years but now the entire world is at peace, thanks be to Allah. There is one people, one faith, and one language.

"Unfortunately, my son, our family resisted the True Faith and the Imams banished us as Nomads, forced to travel the land with no home. After three generations, we understood God's word clearly at last and became one with the Faith. We may now be able to obtain a home and settle. After such a long time, it seems hard to believe our chance has come. We have known no other way of life but that of a Nomad. Soon, you may be able to settle into a school, make friends and get an education, praise be to Allah"

"And Yasmin, too?" Mohammed questioned.

"No, son. You know Yasmin will get her education at home with her mother."

"Oh," he realised his error.

"I tell you all this, son because I want you never to make the mistake our ancestors did. You must always know that Allah is the one True God and you must always be faithful."

Mohammed pondered for a moment, and asked, "Am I allowed to ask what those things we found were?"

"Yes, you may. I discussed it all with our Imam. He said one book, the one with the black cover and the cross on it, was a holy book of an ancient infidel faith. As he said, we had to destroy it to ensure that it would not contaminate people's minds and sway them from the words of Allah. The one with a coloured cover was a children's book of an imaginary story called *The Wizard of Oz*, which can corrupt the minds of the youth with its false tales. The third sheet of paper was an ancient map of this area of our land, which we once called Kansas. Our location is in the southwest corner of it. Our places have different names now.

"We should be happy we live here and may soon get our own home; Allah is the greatest. Much time has passed since those times of the writing of fairy tales, of maps of ancient names, and when the infidels once referred to our Heroes as terrorists.

"Let us be off now to our prayers to Allah and get some much-needed sleep. It has been a long day."

TOMORROW'S NEWSPAPER

I first conceived of the following story in the 1960s and it has gone through seemingly endless edits since. It is about a man who can get a copy of tomorrow's newspaper each day. What would you do if you got a copy?

For many years, Harold J. Goldberg, or Harry to his friends, had been content to be a shoemaker. Now things were not looking quite so well. It used to be that shoemakers made custom-fitted shoes for their customers. If they wore out, the shoemakers repaired them. Those were the good old days when he was always busy. Now that mass production had made shoes so cheap, shoemakers had very few shoes to make anymore. In addition, almost everyone threw their cheap shoes away. For two years now, Harry had been able to stave off bankruptcy. To put the final nail in the coffin of the shoemaker, the continued growth of department stores, and later mass market stores, allowed people to buy shoes more conveniently and cheaply at the same time as they bought most of their other clothes.

"Persistence is the key to success," was Harry's failing motto in a world of change and diversification.

He was born in Germany and was a young boy at the time of the 'Kristallnacht' and the start of the Pogroms. His family immigrated to New York shortly afterwards, escaping in time to avoid the Holocaust. He became a third-generation cobbler under the tutelage of his father and inherited the store after his father passed away when Harry was twenty in 1947. Now, thirty-five years later, he had retained his medium height and slight build. All he had to show for his labours were weathered skin and a slight pot belly. His greying and thinning hair lay on his head in typical disarray. He had piercing eyes inherited from his German mother. Harry's normally robust gait had slowed somewhat and, as he pondered his financial situation, it seemed to slow even more.

He had just passed his thirty-third wedding anniversary. His wife, Alice, had not weathered the years as well as he had. She was two years his junior but three children and diabetes had taken their toll. Her frail constitution was evident in her features. She was thin and sallow. Harry was saddened when he saw her. He deeply loved her and could not picture life without her but he was not a romantic person and had difficulty in showing his love. Even though he had spent his life serving people, he was a shy and quiet person and preferred quiet solitary activities.

Alice was more outgoing and wanted children but her first two children died before they were born. The third child, a girl, had died in early childhood. During the girl's second year of life, she caught pneumonia and succumbed. It happened so fast. One day she was there, the next day she was gone. The death of her little girl destroyed Alice. She was never the same after that. Something inside her had died. She stopped wanting children and Harry was unable to help her. Eventually, even though they loved each other, their respective problems had made them rather distant and quiet.

Harry's shop contained his living quarters on the second floor. He would not have survived financially any other way. To cheer himself up and keep occupied on slow days at the shop, Harry had become engrossed in reading books from the city library or the many second-hand booksellers in town. As business ebbed, he was able to submerge himself in his hobby increasingly.

One evening, Harry sat at his desk by the window in the back of the shop. "Well, I guess that's it. I'll break even again this month," he said almost audibly as he posted his entries for the month. He got up from behind the desk, put on his coat and hat, called to Alice that he was going for a walk, and wandered toward the door as he continued in thought.

"I need something good to read," he mumbled to himself. "I'm tired of the usual bookshops." Then, with a scowl and a sigh, he thought he would try to find a new bookstore. "Maybe I'll find a book I like."

He left his shop and roamed the streets of the city lost in his thoughts. Suddenly, his eye caught a flash of light as he passed what appeared to be an old store of some sort he had not noticed before. The sign he read in the window was rather small, so he would have missed the shop completely if he had not seen the flash of light as it blinked on and off. He had likely missed the shop in the past because he did not usually travel on this street and, when he did, it was always in daylight, so he would easily have missed the sign had it not been for the darkness of night. The sign read:

John's Bookstore Co.
Books Bought and Sold
Old and New

Magazines Newspapers
Oddities and Rarities for the Curious

'Oddities and rarities', he reread. Not very convincing, he thought but he decided to look.

He noticed a small sign on the door saying:

Open
Mon-Thu 9 AM - 5 PM
Fri 9 AM - 8 PM
Sat 10 AM - 4 PM
Sun - Closed

He thought, it's supposed to be closed right now but the light is on.

He pushed the door and it creaked open. He walked in. The store was not impressive and did not appear to be unusual. It was quite ordinary except that it had dim lights and a light layer of dust covering the shelves, which contained rather normal books; mostly paperbacks and magazines. Behind a small counter sat a withered old man dozing in his chair. Harold guessed the man was only ten years older than he was, although the man looked much older.

Harry rummaged through the books available and found nothing noteworthy. "Hey there, mister," he called.

The man stirred in his chair and his eyes opened one at a time. He was small, had grey hair, and wore wireframed glasses. His wrinkled grey suit was a relic. The old man stared at Harry and seemed to be studying him. Finally, he responded, "Shalom."

Harry smiled at the welcome of a fellow Jew and answered with "Shalom," in return.

A squeaky, "Yes, can I help you, sir?" was the old man's drowsy reply.

"I see you're open but the sign on your door shows you're open past your stated hours."

The old man responded, "I thought I'd stay open a little later today."

"I'd like something good to read," Harry announced.

"Well," the man stated in a slow measured pace, "I have a nice selection of books and magazines. Is there anything specific you'd like, or is there any special type of book, perhaps a mystery?"

"Yes, but I've gone through your mystery books and have read them all. Do you have something factual?"

"Well, sir, the non-fiction is over there. The magazines are right beside them. I've got hundreds of National Geographic magazines," the man said as he raised his right arm pointing to the righthand side of the store.

Harry walked through the aisle of books to where the gentleman had motioned. He browsed through the books and magazines as the proprietor anxiously looked on. Eventually, Harry turned to face the owner.

"There's nothing unique here. Have you got something out of the ordinary?"

"Of course, you can see some books beside the magazines, some are first editions."

"No, I looked through those. I want something different, really unusual."

"I don't think I can help you much if you don't like those books. Of course, there's fiction . . ."

"No, I don't want that." Harry interrupted. "I thought you might have something extraordinary."

"Like what?" The dealer leaned forward in his chair.

"I don't know." Harry sighed. "I guess I've read so many books over the years, there's not much left. Well, I guess I'll be going . . ."

Harry turned to go.

"Well, don't you want anything?" the old man pleaded, with the emphasis on the 'anything', anxious for a sale.

"You don't have anything I like that I have not already read."

"Okay, whatever suits you."

"Goodbye," Harry replied as he opened the door to leave. Harry hesitated before taking his first step out the door.

The proprietor mumbled to himself, then called out, "Hey, wait a minute."

Harry stopped in his tracks, let the door slip shut, and turned around to face the dealer who was now standing a few paces from him. The old man peered into Harry's eyes as if trying to search into the depths of his soul.

"Well, what's the matter? Why are you staring at me like that?" Harry asked, suddenly nervous at the oppressive silence.

"I think I may have something for you," the man finally said with satisfaction as to the outcome of his evaluation.

"Like what?" Harry inquired hesitatingly.

"It'll be expensive, though."

"Oh . . . well, let me see it first." He piqued Harry's curiosity. He was unsure as to what the dealer's idea of expensive was but he was also interested in at least looking at what the owner had to offer.

"It's unique, you know," the bookseller stated.

"So, that's good. What is it?"

"You may be a little sceptical because it's so unusual."

"I'm game. First, tell me what it is, then tell me the price." Harry was becoming annoyed.

"It's a difficult thing to tell you about. I'll have to show you." The proprietor went to the back of the store and returned with a newspaper in his hand.

Harry's spirits dropped. "A newspaper? What's so unusual about a newspaper?" Harry said with disgust as he turned to leave, disappointed.

"Just a minute," the old man called out, "at least have a look at it."

Harry spun around. "I've seen the newspaper."

"Look at it, at least."

"What is it, an old paper?"

The old man brought the paper closer to Harry. He held it out so Harry could reach it.

"It looks yellowed. It's an old paper. I'm not a collector of period newspapers." Harry raised his hand, grabbed it, and read the name on it. "Ha, it's *The New York Times*," he scoffed. "What's so different about that? It's our local paper." Harry thrust it back to the bookseller.

"Look carefully." The old man was now getting annoyed with Harry's lack of perceptiveness.

Harry pulled it in and looked again. "Headlines, index . . . So, what's the diff . . . hey, wait a minute, it says November 8, 1982, and today's the seventh. They must have goofed on the date . . . Today's the seventh, isn't it?"

"No goof, the date on the paper is right and today is indeed the seventh." The old man was now smiling. "Have you seen those news articles before?"

Harry quickly scanned the headlines further but when he started to flip through the pages, the edge snapped off a page. He moved to a small table in the centre of the shop, set the paper on top of it and flipped through a few pages. He could only open it with great care. A careful examination of it showed the print was much lighter than normal and the paper indeed had yellowed and was quite brittle. "No . . . but this must be a hoax. What printer sells tomorrow's newspapers? This paper looks as if it's fifty years old, so how can it have tomorrow's date? The news looks as if it could come from tomorrow, some of the articles are follow-ups to some articles I read today but the whole thing doesn't make sense," Harry said aloud.

"This isn't a joke. I just get them. Now, I'm trying to sell one to you. They come in almost every day. As far as I know, I'm the only person in the world who gets them. I'm sort of exclusive, I guess."

Harry was sceptical. The man must be kidding. "If this is tomorrow's newspaper, wouldn't you be selling a lot of them?"

"Possibly but I wouldn't sell it to anyone."

Harry stood up, turned to leave, hesitated, then thought better of it, and proceeded to go out the door. Hundreds of questions crowded his mind. Would anybody not just love to read tomorrow's newspaper? Then it dawned on him, that if someone did regularly get tomorrow's newspaper, he could become rich quite quickly. If . . . but then, it was quite impossible. Then again, if tomorrow's newspaper could be so helpful to a person, why had the owner of the bookstore not taken advantage of the possibilities himself, and why did the paper look so old?

He finally reached the door to his shop. He unlocked the door, opened it, entered, locked the door then slowly climbed the stairs to his tiny apartment. His wife was sitting in her rocking chair, knitting. He greeted her with a kiss on the cheek and ambled to his room. He got ready for bed and searched his bookshelves for something to read. There was nothing he wanted to reread. He slid into the bed and finally slipped into a restless sleep.

The next morning, he was cooking breakfast when he heard the paper clatter against the door. After he finished cooking, he wandered down to collect the paper to read while he ate.

He bounded up the stairs, sat down to breakfast, and opened his paper. He gaped at the first page. He flipped through a few other pages. He could not be sure but the paper looked familiar. It looked as if it was the same one that he had perused quickly the night before.

He mumbled . . . "that guy got an advance copy of the paper. He must have but the paper doesn't go to press until midnight, so how did he get it?"

His wife entered to join him for breakfast. She noticed his confusion. "What's the matter?" she asked, as she grabbed the egg carton.

"I'm not sure yet."

"Oh . . . can I help with anything?" She cracked two eggs into the frying pan and popped a slice of bread into the toaster.

He paused then said, "Yes, you could look after the store while I go out for a while later this morning."

"I hope there's nothing wrong?" she asked.

"No, actually it may be something good. I shouldn't be long," he affirmed.

He finished his meal, put his dishes into the sink, and pecked his wife on the cheek as he passed her on the way to the stairs. At nine o'clock, he opened his shop. Only two people came in to leave their shoes for repair. His mind, however, was not on his work. He kept thinking about that newspaper. By noon, he could take it no longer. He slung the day's paper under his arm, told Alice he was going out for a while, and hustled over to the bus stop.

He got off the bus near the bookstore and hurried to its door. He opened it and entered. The old man was sitting with his eyes closed near the back of the store. "Shalom," Harry opened.

The proprietor opened first one eye, then the other. "Oh, shalom. Back again, are you?"

"Yeah, I need some answers." Harry flung his paper onto the small counter in front of the man.

"Yeah?"

"Do you still have the paper you tried to sell me yesterday?"

"Sure, here it is." The old man reached under his counter and pulled it out.

Harry took it and went over to the table where he could open it up for comparison with the paper that he had received that morning. He compared the two papers page by page. They were identical.

"Okay, how did you do it?" Harry almost snarled.

"Do what?"

"Get tomorrow's paper before it comes out?"

"It's a rather long story."

"I'm all ears."

"I don't know enough about you to tell you the whole story now. Let's just say, through some quirk of nature, I'm able to get tomorrow's newspaper."

"If you can get a paper like this you must know you can make a lot of money knowing tomorrow's news. Why didn't you take advantage of it? You could be doing quite well knowing the news the day before it happens."

"I know. I've tried it. After a time, I realised knowing tomorrow's news isn't so great. I got a little afraid of knowing too much. Now, I wouldn't even look at it."

"You've got to be kidding. If this is true, just think of the things you could do with tomorrow's news."

"Not what I could do, what you could do. You could use it for great good, or great evil. I'm taking a big chance to let you in on my secret. When I saw you yesterday, I could see by your dress you were a man of little means. I could also see something else in you, enough for me to make you the offer I did."

A very serious look now showed on Harry's face as he asked, "How much do you want for the next issue?"

"I've given it a lot of thought. I'm up to my eyes in debt. This place is ready to fall on my head. I don't know you too well. I'm not long for this world . . . I'll say . . . 1000 dollars."

"What? 1000 dollars for a crummy newspaper? What is this, a gag?"

"Not just a crummy newspaper, tomorrow's newspaper."

Harry thought about it. If he did have tomorrow's newspaper, it would be worth much more if he used the paper to its full advantage. If it was a fake though, then it was a high price for an almost bankrupt shoemaker. "I don't have that kind of money," he finally responded.

"Sorry then, I'm a businessperson. I can't give it away."

"Do you have tomorrow's paper now?"

"Sorry, no. You get the money for tomorrow, cash, or certified cheque, and I'll have the next day's paper for you. I have the bank on my back and if I don't get them fixed up, I may not have the shop much longer. I won't accept less than 1000 dollars."

Harry thought about it. Where was he going to get the money? He could perhaps ask this guy to give him the first copy in good faith for later payment but Harry would not do that. No, this was a business transaction and he would find the money himself.

Harry finally spoke, "I'm a poor man myself but I'll get it for you."

The proprietor smiled.

"When can I pick up the paper?"

"Come around ten o'clock tomorrow morning and I'll have it for you." The book dealer had a strange smile as if he were guarding a deep secret.

"Shalom . . ." Harry said as he slowly turned to leave. He had a long day ahead of him.

"Shalom," responded the shopkeeper, as Harry walked out the door.

Harry hopped onto the bus and headed home. He needed money, and quickly. He also needed money to invest to get money to pay for the next day's paper. A bank was out of the question. They would never lend money to a near bankrupt. He thought about the friends he had, and who might have 2000 dollars available.

After much consideration, he settled on his old friend Charley Goldstein. Harry had never asked anyone for money before and he felt very uncomfortable. He called Charley on the telephone as soon as he reached home. He had to be evasive about why he needed the money and he promised to pay it back in a couple of weeks. The only thing was, that Charley did not have 2000 dollars. He could scrape up only fifteen hundred dollars but it would have to do. Harry would be able to pick it up at six o'clock that evening.

When he hung up the phone, he felt humiliated. The thought of borrowing from a friend repulsed him. He knew well the Shakespearian adage on the subject. What he feared most was the thought, that if this did not work, the same curse would befall him. He had known Charley since elementary school and he was not interested in losing him as a friend for any amount of money.

He picked up the day's paper again and searched for ideas about what he could do to make some fast money. He formulated his plan. There was a football game the next day. He would use that as his springboard for now.

At five-thirty, he hopped on the bus to Charley's. He was back before seven o'clock. He put the money into an envelope and placed it into the drawer of his desk.

He was restless that night. He thought it was too good to be true. He feared something would go wrong. How could a person be so lucky?

Morning finally arrived. He rose early and made breakfast. and sat down to eat. He heard the familiar noise of the paper's arrival and went down to the door to pick it up. He spent the next hour reading and trying to get himself organised for the next couple of days.

Just before nine-thirty, Harry asked Alice to mind the shop while he was out. He pulled out the packet of money from his desk drawer and counted out 1000 dollars. He placed the money into a new envelope. He returned the remaining five hundred dollars into the old envelope, placed it back into the drawer and left the shop. He walked to the bus stop and was soon on the bus to the bookstore. He got there just after ten o'clock.

He entered and spotted the familiar face at the back of the shop. "Shalom," he opened.

The older man was awake this time and glanced up. "Oh, Shalom, you're ready for your paper? I was expecting you. Do you have the money?"

"I said I'd get it," John responded.

"Let's see it."

Harry handed over the envelope and said, "It's all there." He felt as if he were doing something criminal, although he was breaking no human law. He was doing something impossible; he was breaking a natural law.

The man took a quick look at its contents. "Looks like it. Here's your paper." The old man reached under the counter and pulled out a yellowed newspaper.

Harry reached out as if he were receiving a bar of gold and took it. He looked at the top of the front page. Yes, it had tomorrow's date. "Still don't want to tell me how you got this?"

"Sorry, no . . ." the proprietor responded resolutely.

"At least you can tell me why it looks so old."

"That can be part of the mystery."

Harry turned to leave. The shopkeeper added, "Oh, by the way, you have to promise two things."

"What?" Harry spun around to face the man.

"Don't tell me any news in the newspapers about me and don't tell anyone about this. Can you imagine what would happen if someone else found out I could supply someone with a copy of tomorrow's newspaper?"

"Oh?"

"Just don't. Promise?"

"Okay, suit yourself. I wouldn't want anyone else to know, for sure. I wouldn't want to jeopardise a good thing for me."

Harry looked at the man as he folded the newspaper. Somehow, he felt this must be a fraud. Something inside, though, was screaming at him to get out and carefully examined his prize. He had nothing, so he had nothing to lose.

"I have another question," Harry blurted out. "Is this paper guaranteed?"

The store owner looked askance and replied, "The only guarantee I can give you is, it's tomorrow's newspaper. If you determine it is not identical to the paper you will find at the newsstand tomorrow, I'll give you your money back. I'm not going anywhere. What you do with the information you see in the paper is up to you."

The old man noticed Harry begin to turn to leave. "By the way, as we've formed a business arrangement, friends call me, John."

Harry paused, then swung out his right hand and responded, "Name's Harry, pleased to do business with you."

Before he released Harry's hand, John added, "Occasionally, I don't get the newspaper, so to avoid your having to come here for nothing on those days, please give me your phone number and I'll call you."

Harry was puzzled but wrote his phone number on a slip of paper John gave him, then turned around and walked out of the store. He kept pondering the situation. He had scanned the paper but could he trust it? If it proved not to be tomorrow's newspaper, he would have to get the money back from the bookstore owner but still, he would be out five hundred dollars for the wager he was about to make with Charley's money. He knew what he was planning to do but it relied on the information in the paper.

I'd better do things slowly, he thought to himself. This paper is untried yet.

When he arrived at his shop, he alerted Alice he was back. He went to his desk at the rear of the store, opened the paper, and leafed through the sports pages. "Ah, what a secret," he whispered. He opened the desk drawer, pulled out the envelope with the five hundred dollars and put it in his pocket.

Next, he dialled the number of a bookie and placed a five hundred dollar bet on a football game the bookie noted had a score with ten-to-one odds. He called upstairs to tell Alice he would be out for a few minutes again and asked her to look after things while he was gone. He left the shop and caught a bus. He dropped the money off with the bookie and returned to the shop. While repairing the few shoes that he had left for repair, he listened to the football game on the radio. The score appeared in the newspaper. After supper, he picked up his 5,000 winnings and hid them in an envelope in his desk drawer.

That night, he felt wonderful. He had waited for a break in his life for a long time now. He was tired but found it hard to sleep because of the excitement. He was already considering his options for tomorrow.

Alice had noticed his excitement and enquired as to its source but Harry considered it prudent not to give her too many details. He just said he had won some money on a bet on a football game.

The next morning, he rose early, dressed, and had breakfast. He heard the clatter of the paper on the doorstep outside of the store. He smiled, went to the door, opened it, and picked up the paper. He took a long, satisfied look at the front page. A quick look at the rest of it assured him all was well. It was identical to the paper he had received the day before. He folded it and deposited it in the garbage. Later in the day, he cancelled his subscription, as he would not need it anymore.

He went to his desk drawer and pulled out the envelope with yesterday's winnings. He counted out the 1000 dollars needed for tomorrow's newspaper and slid it into an envelope. Around 9:30, he walked to the bus stop and caught a bus to the bookstore. He was cheerful as he entered it to make his greeting and purchase.

He returned to his shop and reviewed the results of that day's horse races. He decided not to bet on the low-odds races but concentrate on the three long-shot winners for the day. That would give him the largest winnings without attracting too much notice. If he won every race, someone may get suspicious. He made his notes.

In the afternoon, he splurged by taking a taxi to the racetrack. Placing his bets and walking away with his winnings was just too easy.

He got home a little later than he planned. Alice greeted him with many questions as to his whereabouts. She had gotten worried. These absences from home lately were very uncharacteristic of him. She was surprised at where he had been. Harry had rarely gambled before and now this was the second consecutive day he had done this. She was glad he had won so much money but not happy about how he had gotten it.

Harry knew he could not gamble often, primarily because of Alice's concerns but also because of the suspicions his activities may arouse from the bookies or the racetrack officials.

He decided to bolster his knowledge of stock trading to see what he could do there. One day's notice was not enough time to make investment decisions but it may allow him to make quick trades. He opened a trading account with a nearby broker and spent the last part of the evening examining the financial pages of the previous papers.

In the morning, he went to the bookstore, bought his paper, and returned home. He read that a company was going to make a deal later that day on a large order for its products. He went to his broker and put all his spare cash into that company's shares.

Later that day, the announcement came, as expected, and the shares went up. He sold half his shares to have money for the next transaction. He picked up his paper the next day and noted the share's price had increased again. He also saw another stock was going to climb, so he bought into that one, too.

By the end of the week, he was doing well trading in puts and calls. His broker was amazed at his prowess.

One evening, he sauntered over to his desk and sat down. For several minutes, he sat and stared into open space. He leaned over, picked up the phone and called a realtor to tell him he was closing his shop and wanted to sell. The realtor would draw up the documents right away, and he would review and sign them the next day.

Alice was quite shocked when Harry told her about his actions. She worried that his luck would run out, leaving them with nothing to fall back on.

Harry explained that the shop was not profitable and had not been for years. Selling it would let him pay his debts faster. They could take the money they could get from it and buy a house, where they could semi-retire as he flourished in his new career. It took him some time to convince Alice but he showed her how the stock market worked and how he could be successful in picking winning sports teams or racehorses. In the end, he won her over. He had also avoided violating his promise to John.

The next day, he visited Charley and gave him 15,000 dollars in repayment for the loan. Charley did not want the extra money but Harry was very insistent. He told Charley he had made a lot of money and Charley should share his good luck.

The next day, he paid off all his small loans and made payments on the others. Harry thought it would keep his creditors at bay for a while.

One day, he got a call from John telling him there was no paper to pick up. He would not say why. The next day, the paper was there as usual. From time to time, Harry would receive a call that there was no paper for him.

So, it went, day after day, week after week, until he had paid all his debts and became a millionaire. He was a very busy man. He moved into a nice new bungalow so Alice would not have to climb stairs and indulged in a limousine with a chauffeur and a house cleaner. He even rented an office near his broker.

A few years passed. Harry was sitting in his office with his coffee in his hand perusing the paper. "Let's see now, stocks, good," he mumbled. He made a few notes. He was about to close the paper when an article caught his eye. The heading said, "Wife of Local Millionaire Dies". He read further.

"Oh, no! Not Alice," he mumbled, "It can't be but it must be. He read further, 'dies of natural causes'". What do I do? he thought. What do I say? Should I tell her? Maybe I should not but then again should she not know? I must do something.

He sat motionless while his brain raced. He thought about his life with her. How could he live without her? Lately, he had noticed she was a little more listless than usual. Was this the warning?

Finally, he snapped out of his stupor and rushed home. His chauffeur was a little irritated by his urging for speed. He jumped out of the car before it came to a full stop.

"Alice?" he shouted, as he threw open the front door.

"Yes dear?" she replied as she hurried to the door to greet him.

"Alice, I . . ." He did not know what to say.

"What?" she asked anxiously as she could detect from the tone of his voice that something was wrong.

"Oh, nothing . . ." He stared at the wall to the left of her.

"Don't hide anything from me. You're upset about something."

He froze. His brain wanted to say something but his mouth would not respond. "Let's go out on the town. Just you and I," he finally blurted.

"I have nothing special to do today. I'd love to but you don't look as if you're in a particularly good mood right now."

"Oh? No, everything is okay," he lied.

"Where do you want to go?"

Harry knew she had only about six hours to live and it was noon. "Let's go somewhere quiet for lunch. We can start from there."

He grabbed her coat quickly, put it on her, and rushed her out the door. He could not give her time to think. He could not give himself time to think. He helped her into the car.

They sat in the back of their limousine while Harry kept her talking. He took her to a fancy restaurant for lunch. He let the chauffeur return home. They left the restaurant and began walking through Central Park while talking about their life together.

"Isn't it beautiful here?" Alice broke in.

Harry looked around and had to admit she was right. "It sure is," he agreed.

"It's like a touch of country in the middle of the city."

Harry did not respond. He soaked in what she had said.

They walked in relative silence enjoying each other's company arm-in-arm until after five o'clock.

She finally announced, "I'm getting awfully tired. My legs are aching. I haven't walked like this in a long time."

"It's only after five." He hoped, that if they kept active, she would miss her date with death.

"Maybe we should go home now," she stammered.

"Let's rest for a while first then I'll take you to a nice restaurant for supper."

They sat down on a bench beside the path. Harry was also getting tired and out of breath. The quiet walk had eased his nerves but the idea of her death was rising again to obsess him. His nervousness became even more evident. Guilt overpowered him, as he thought about their life together. He could not rid himself of the idea that maybe he had not given her enough, especially love. He realised how much he loved her.

Alice was now convinced something was wrong. "Harry, is something wrong with the business? Are stocks going to fall? You look terrible tonight," she uttered in a low, tired, and slightly raspy tone.

Harry did not answer. He racked his brain trying to think of what would please her most but he did not know. She had always been happy with anything he gave her and he had always been too busy with work, his reading, or other things, especially before he started getting tomorrow's newspapers, to find out. In his dazed state, Harry forgot about time.

Harry looked at his watch. A shiver ran up and down his spine. How could he stop what he knew must happen but he knew it had been in the paper and the paper was always right?

Finally, he turned to Alice. "Okay Alice, let's go home." There was no response. "Alice?"

He looked at his watch again. It was after six o'clock. He looked back at Alice frozen on the bench, her chin resting on her chest and her eyes staring blindly at the sidewalk. The newspaper had won. He leaned over and kissed her on her cheek. Uncontrollably, his eyes filled with tears. He was not the sentimental type and had had many hardships in his life. He had gone through the death of his father and mother. He had learned not to cry and here he was . . . but it was Alice, and it was too much to bear.

When he regained his senses, he got up, walked slowly down the path to the street, and called for help. A passer-by called an ambulance, which took Alice to the hospital's emergency room.

Harry paced back and forth in the hospital's waiting room. A man approached him and told him he was a reporter for *The New York Times* and he wanted to get the details of what had happened. Harry told his story and the reporter disappeared to post his article for the next day's newspaper.

In the emergency room, a doctor checked Alice over and confirmed her death. He made a couple of phone calls and then went to the waiting room to talk to Harry.

"Did she have to die?" Harry blubbered as he stood up. "She wasn't that old . . . I mean . . . she had some life ahead of her, didn't she?" He knew he was not making much sense and his voice was cracking, and his eyes were moistening again.

The physician answered, "She died of natural causes from what I can determine, probably a chronic heart ailment. I contacted her doctor and found out she hadn't been to his office in quite some time."

"She didn't like doctors," Harry blurted out. "She was afraid of them. I tried to get her to go several times for a check-up but I didn't want to force her. I thought she was okay."

"If she'd seen him, she might have been put on medication and avoided what happened. In addition, her low iron level indicated she was anaemic. You said you went on a long walk this afternoon?"

Harry nodded.

The doctor continued, "That might have been a contributing factor. Your wife wasn't exactly a strong person or in good health."

Harry stood there, speechless. He felt a strangeness he could not explain. He was trying to piece together what had happened. This confusion led to his becoming afraid but afraid of what? Would she still be alive if he had not learned of her death in the paper? What if he had taken her to a doctor instead of going for a walk?

It was months before he could deal with his mourning. Going through her possessions and selling them or giving them away was agony for him. He kept some mementoes for himself. He finally learned to accept her death.

Then, about two years later, another issue presented itself. He was on his way to the bookshop as usual with thoughts of what he had to do. His limousine stopped in front of the store. Harry climbed out of it and entered the shop.

"Shalom, John, here's your 1000 dollars."

"Thanks," the old shopkeeper replied while handing him the paper.

"Shalom," Harry said as he walked out of the store and started flipping through the pages. He got into the limousine and the driver drove off.

Harry scanned through the obituaries. "Oh, no, Charley's going to die," he muttered, then raised his voice, "Driver, take me to Charley Falstaff's."

"Yes, sir."

Harry remembered Charley had asked him to tell him if he knew when Charley was going to die. Now he would have to tell him. Charley had come to know that Harry had developed some way of looking into the future but keeping his promise to the bookseller, Harry had never told Charley his secret.

Harry's driver drove him to the front of a small house in an older section of town. The trees surrounding the house were in full bloom and beautiful to see. He plopped the paper onto the car seat, got out of the car, walked to the front door, and hesitated. Wild thoughts about Alice ran through his head but he knew Charley wanted to know.

He was trying to decide whether to ring the doorbell or not when the door opened. A little old man stood on the other side of it. His scalp was almost bald, the years showed on his face. Harry saw it as a mirror of himself. That once-upon-a-time young boy looked so old and frail. Harry thought it strange that, even though they met regularly, he had never noticed his age, nor seen the deterioration over the years. As parents notice changes in their growing children through the eyes of others, he is now seeing Charley for what he was, and through him, seeing himself. Like Charley, he too had grown old.

"Saw you coming through the window." Charley broke his thoughts.

Harry looked at Charley and down at the doorsill in front of him.

"Well, don't stand there, come on in." Charley added, "There's always room for an old friend inside."

Harry slowly took the offer and entered the house. He went to where Charley was motioning him to sit down. He sat down as a man with a huge burden and fell heavily into the old chair.

Charley sat across from him. "Nice to see you, Harry. I haven't seen you since the day before yesterday." With this, Charley gave out a slight snicker. Charley was always the joker.

Harry answered seriously, "Yeah, Shalom, Charley."

"Well, is that all you're going to say? Is something the matter, Harry? Why the glum expression?"

"The day has come, Charley," Harry stammered.

"The day has what?" Charley responded, puzzled.

"Has come — the day of reckoning." Harry did not know what else to say.

The old man began to shake nervously. "You mean it's time?" Charley asked softly.

"Yes, I didn't want to tell you. You wanted to know, though," Harry said reluctant.

"Yeah, sure, I told you . . . are you sure, I mean . . . are you positive?"

"Have I been wrong before, Charley?" Harry asked firmly.

Charley looked deeply into Harry's eyes. "No, not lately."

"I never wanted to say this to you, Charley. You know what happened with Alice."

"Shame, what a shame. You must still miss her. I knew how much you loved her but I've lived my life, Harry. I'm scared, though. I mean what happens after? Is it a trip to somewhere else or just a fleeting moment in time?" He sat in silence for several minutes. "I guess I'd better make sure I'm ready."

"You're a good guy, Charley."

"It seems only yesterday when we were kids, huh, Harry?"

"Yeah."

"My, how time passes, then, before you know it, you're old. Heck, I don't feel that old. We've talked so much about the old days." Charley was getting ready to leave and reached over to pick up his sweater. "Well . . . goodbye Harry. I sort of hate to go but I've got lots to do today – lots of loose ends to tie up. In a way, I'm lucky. I know few people can close the books on their life. It's like writing the last chapter of your life, the last page."

"Yeah, I understand. Is there anything I can do? I'd do anything, old friend. Do you want me to stay?"

"No . . . I'm fine, Harry . . . This is something I'd like to do alone."

Harry got up and began walking toward the door. He did not know what else to do, or to say. He could think of many things he would want to do with him but he felt now that Charley would want to be alone to do things as he saw fit. As he reached the door, he turned to his friend who was just steps behind him. "Goodbye, Charley."

Charley could see the sadness in Harry's eyes. "Ah, come on, Harry, everything is going to be okay. Just think that I've gone on a trip. Someday we'll be together again. So, see you again, Harry."

Charley approached his old friend and gave him a warm hug.

"Not too often you get to write your obituary. I can even put it in the paper in advance. How many people can get to put their obituary in the paper before they die? Heck, it'll be in tomorrow's newspaper. By the way Harry, how does it happen, or are you able to say?"

"Yes, quietly in your sleep."

"Good, that's what I'll put in my obituary."

Harry turned and walked over to the car. He watched as Charley hurried down the street to take care of what he wanted to do before it was all over. When Charley was no longer in view, Harry opened the car door and got in. When he returned home, he ended the day in drink. The next morning, he alerted the police to check Charley's home.

He went to Charley's funeral. Charley had not left much to the world and he had given what he had to charity but Harry buried him in style. Charley had never married and died as he lived, alone.

Harry was not the same after that. The death of Alice had been traumatic but now it was his best friend, someone who had been with him since the first day he had moved to New York. Being almost the same age, with very much the same disposition, they had even done their bar mitzvah together. They had been inseparable.

Business continued as usual but his heart was not in it. Day after day, week after week, Harry continued in his despondent way. He started to gain weight but continued to make his almost daily trip to the bookstore.

John had remodelled the bookstore by now. It was quite modern but retained an air of oldness about it. The aged owner was not a big spender but had updated his wardrobe and had managed to put aside a small fortune.

One day, Harry entered as he had always done. "Shalom, John."

"You don't look good, Harry. For the last few months, you've looked terrible," John responded as he handed over the paper.

"Yeah, I've got the flu." Harry handed him the envelope of money.

"What kind of flu, the twenty-four-month flu? You've been like this for several months now. I've kept it to myself until now. I mind my own business but I can't hold back anymore. You come, buy the paper then go hardly saying a word. You're turning into a nervous wreck."

"I can't help it."

"Talk – maybe that'll help."

"I don't think that'll help. After all these years you've never changed your price for the newspaper. 1000 dollars isn't worth as much as when we made our agreement. I've offered you more but you won't take it."

"Who needs more? I've got all I need. I get 1000 dollars a day for almost every day of the year, and I have peace of mind. I don't think you have the same."

Harry slid out a chair beside the counter, sat on it and thought. A question that had bothered him since the beginning of their arrangement resurrected itself. "Who sells you the papers?"

"I've told you before."

"No, you didn't. You talked in circles and said it was none of my business."

"I didn't say it that way."

"Well, that's the way I understood it."

"Now, don't speak hastily. It's just very hard to explain."

"Explain what?"

"Well . . . nothing."

"Look, I've been coming here for years now. I'm entitled to know."

"Why should I tell you? If you get it, why should that question bother you?"

"Why not? If someone was giving you tomorrow's newspaper, wouldn't you wonder where he got it, hours before it was published, and hours before most of the events happened?"

There was a long silence as Harry stared at John as he sat in a chair next to him.

"Will you keep it to yourself then?" There was another pause. "As I said before, I don't want scientists and news people swarming over my place. It may be hard to explain because I'm not sure I understand it myself."

"Well, go on."

"Will you understand it though?"

"You won't know until you try, will you."

"That's a fact. What exactly do you want to know then?"

"Just start from the beginning. I'll keep it to myself."

"Okay . . . when I first bought this place many years ago, it was in almost the same shape as when you first came in here. At first, I used both the lower and upper floors for displaying books but about three years before I met you, sales had dropped substantially so I reduced the number of books I carried and moved from my apartment to live on the second floor of the shop. That floor had a washroom, kitchen, and bedroom area, as people had used it as an upper apartment long before I bought the place. I figured I could save some money and I didn't need a large place to live, especially after my wife died. It also meant I wouldn't have to commute anymore, and that would save me more money.

"Anyway, one morning I woke up and went to the kitchen to make breakfast and read the paper. I took a shower, dressed, and opened the store at nine o'clock. About one hour later, I went upstairs to go to the washroom. When I passed the night table, I noticed a newspaper sitting on it. I didn't remember putting it there. I don't know how long I stood there before I finally reached out and picked it up, although I had to be careful, as it was so brittle and yellowed. I laid the paper on the bed and flipped through the pages. I hadn't read the articles before, although some of the articles seemed to be follow-ups to those I had read earlier in the morning. I was puzzled as to why I would place a paper I had not read on the night table.

"I picked up the yellowed paper, folded it, went downstairs and shoved it under my counter. It turned out to be a slow day and I thought more about that yellowed paper. I picked it up from behind the counter and examined it more closely. I checked the date on it. I knew then something was crazy and didn't make sense. It had the next day's date on it – tomorrow's date. I was puzzled about the yellowing and brittleness of the paper. Why should it look old? I placed the paper back behind the counter.

"I didn't sleep well that night and woke up tired. When I heard the clatter of the paper on the doorstep, I went downstairs and brought it upstairs to read in bed. Some of the articles seemed familiar; because I was certain I had seen them in the yellowed paper yesterday. I placed the newspaper on the night table and dozed off for about an hour. I took my shower, dressed for the day, and noticed the night table was bare. I looked around the room but couldn't find it anywhere. I left the bedroom, made breakfast, ate, and went downstairs to open the store. When I went upstairs around noon, I passed the door to my bedroom door and saw something on the night table. On closer examination, I saw it was another yellowed paper with the next day's date on it. During lunch, I read the articles. All I could think about for the rest of the day were those two papers that had appeared on the night table. I developed a plan for the next day.

"On the next morning, I picked up the day's newspaper and placed it on my night table. I sat on the bed and watched it. Around 7:30, the paper started to shimmer, then it disappeared. I made breakfast and ate my food facing the door to my bedroom, so I could continue to watch the night table. I decided not to open the store at 9 o'clock, as I usually did not have many if any, customers at that time in the morning anyway. Finally, at about 9:15, the tabletop shimmered and a yellowed paper appeared on it.

"I continued placing each day's newspapers onto the table and reading the next day's papers for several weeks. I could see the possibilities of getting the next day's paper but I didn't take advantage of it. I was afraid. I learned about earthquakes, floods, and deaths before they happened and felt horrible. I couldn't do anything about them without letting officials know about the strange phenomenon in my room. I had no interest in making money from the papers if I had to deal with the other news items too.

"I'm not sure how the transfer process works. The day's paper disappears with a shimmer between seven and eight o'clock and the next day's paper arrives in a shimmer around nine to ten o'clock. Almost every time I saw tomorrow's paper, I had placed the next day's paper onto the night table.

"One day, there was no paper on the table. The next morning, I was nervous about continuing with the paper. I decided to stop it. I never put a paper on the table again . . . until the day after you came to the store."

"Do you have any more ideas about it?" asked Harry.

"I don't know. It might be that the area above the table is some type of time warp, wormhole, or something like that. That's hard to understand though, because that anomaly would have to follow Earth's orbit at the same velocity as the Earth, so it might tie into the Earth's orbit somehow, or it might be a gravitational anomaly. I'm not a scientist, so I wouldn't know. I consider it a miracle and leave it at that. I suspect the site also gets unstable at times. That would explain why sometimes we do not get a paper, and it seems to be doing that more now than it has in the past. You may have noticed it's getting less predictable. Someday, this anomaly may end and there'll be no more tomorrow's newspaper."

There was another pause then Harry asked, "What about the previous owner?"

"Well, there's no telling when this started. It may have been before I put the night table there, or it may have been there for years. The previous owner had no furniture where the table is now and he never said anything about it."

Harry sat soaking in all he had heard. He was not sure he understood the whole thing but he understood enough to know it did work. "What about the weathering of the paper?"

"I have no idea. The paper moves backwards in time, so the time shift must affect the paper." The old man continued. "I hope you'll continue to keep this between you and me. I don't want anybody else to know about it. If they do, then you can imagine what could happen."

"Yes, I can guess. Why did you offer the paper to me?"

"As I said, I found a paper on the table the morning you came into the shop. That meant the next morning I would put a paper on the table. The only reason for me to do that would be if someone had come along to buy it. When you came, I guessed you were the one and wouldn't spread the fact that I could sell someone tomorrow's newspaper. I had two other people come in that day but I could sense it wasn't them. I usually closed the shop earlier than you arrived but as you may remember, I kept the shop open still waiting for that person to come, and then there you were."

"Very interesting. Thanks for your story. Now I know why you were so interested in keeping the paper secret."

They said their goodbyes and Harry left the old shop. Somehow, fate had been with him. It was meant to be that he received these papers. What his future held . . . he would only know a day in advance.

Several months passed relatively uneventfully for Harry. One day, John told him he wanted to retire. Harry made a deal to buy the property. Now, it was Harry who had to take over the chore of leaving a paper on the night table. Harry closed the store to the public but left it standing as it always had – books and all.

It was bound to happen. When he saw the article, he had to read it over again. It was about a man who had committed suicide. Harry forced himself to check the name a second time. It was the John he knew as the bookstore owner.

Why would he have committed suicide, he thought? What probable reason could he have had for killing himself? Why didn't he die a natural death? After all, he was an old man.

Harry spent the whole morning trying to figure it out. By lunch, he had no conclusive idea in mind. He kept wondering if he should tell John to warn him of what was to happen. Everything seemed so confusing. If he went to John, he might get angry and commit suicide but then again, maybe he was planning to commit suicide and Harry could convince him not to do it but anything he did would end up with the same result – John would kill himself. The paper was the proof.

He decided not to tell John about it but resolved to visit him to determine his state of mind and decide on a course of action. He had himself driven to John's condominium and knocked on the door. The door opened.

"Shalom," Harry began.

"Shalom," John replied. They shook hands warmly.

"How are you doing?" Harry asked, trying to hide his knowledge.

"All right, I guess. Retirement has been good for me. Come on in. May I make you some coffee?"

Harry entered and sat down on a nearby chair John had pointed out to him. "No, thanks."

"What brings you to my place?" John continued.

"Just a visit. I just wanted to see how you were doing. Do you need anything?"

"No, I'm doing fine. I still have a lot of savings, if that's what you mean. I'll be able to help my children when I go. I'm going to have a very big funeral one of these days," John said as he sat in another chair.

Harry could hardly hide his reaction to this statement. The old man must have sensed Harry's unease.

"What's bothering you, Harry? You don't seem yourself today."

"Ah, nothing."

John looked intensely into Harry's eyes. He could probably see the answer there.

"I don't think you should have come here, Harry. I know you can tell what's going to happen. You're acting very strangely. If the reason is what I think it is, then you shouldn't have come here today."

Harry responded embarrassedly. "Sorry."

"You've got something to say?"

"Forget it. I just came on a friendly visit to find out how you were."

John stared at Harry. He knew what was there. He could detect the increase in Harry's nervousness. "You have ruined everything, you know. I didn't want to know. That was one of the reasons why I stopped reading the paper because I feared the day that I'd see my obituary, or some other personal tragedy coming up," John yelled.

At that, John stood and raced out of his home before Harry could get a chance to stop him or explain.

"Hey, stop. Wait. You don't know how. You don't understand." Harry ran to the door but John was already too far up the street. Harry knew it was useless to follow him, and found himself in a severe state of shock. He walked back to the nearby chair and sat down.

"The fool, he doesn't understand. He doesn't know how it will happen," he mumbled to himself.

Harry got up and returned home. There was nothing he could do.

He had a fitful sleep. In the morning, he went over to the bookstore. He waited until noon but no paper arrived on the night table. Harry strode out of the bookstore and his chauffeur took him back home. He sauntered inside. Now, he was alone. His parents had both died many years ago. He had no brothers, sisters, aunts, uncles, wives, children, best friends, and now a business associate. Sure, he had his employees but it was not the same. He sat down on a chair and wept.

Harry was torn in two. Tomorrow's newspaper had helped him and ruined him. Was he determining his future or was tomorrow's newspaper deciding it? Would Alice have died, if he had never seen tomorrow's newspaper? Would John have committed suicide, or would these things have happened anyway? It was an endless loop, a Mobius strip. He did it; the newspaper did it. The paper did it; he did it. Did it possess him, or did he possess it?

He cancelled his subscription to the newspaper and did not go back to the bookstore.

For months, the bookstore stood unvisited, just the table, the building, and the books, empty, like Harry. Harry had had it. He did not think about the paper anymore. He could live well on his fortune. He did not need the papers. All he wanted was to keep the building from anybody else. Finally, he decided he had to demolish it. The city had been after him since he bought it to either use it or get rid of it. It was an old firetrap.

He got the demolition permit for it and contracted for the wreckers. He wanted to supervise the event. The first few days, he saw the books removed and the building's insides taken out. The workers stripped every moveable item from the inside – except the night table. That happened to be one of the last items remaining before they levelled the building.

Harry was regenerating his health and losing weight. A load had lifted from him. He had planned a long vacation. He was going to take a world tour – maybe that would make him feel better. He went over to the bookstore in the morning before its demolition to see how it was progressing. It had almost finished. He walked around the empty hulk, remembering the many times he had entered the place, almost every day for so many years now.

He glanced at the small table against the wall and then stopped. He turned his eyes away, then toward it again. He looked closer. His eyes were not what they used to be but there was something on it. He walked slowly toward it. It was a yellowed newspaper. He wondered how it had gotten there. It could only be tomorrow's paper, or it would not have been there and would not have yellowed.

He realised that he could not the paper there so he picked it up, folded it, and tucked it under his arm. On the way home, he kept wondering why the paper was there. Did he stop the demolition and start putting the papers back on the table? How? The table was not supposed to be there tomorrow!

He returned home and sat down in his big easy chair. He put the folded paper down on the coffee table next to him. His head turned toward it. This would be the last time he would ever have a chance to read it, he thought. Once the workers destroyed the building, that would be it.

He put on his glasses, reached over, picked it up and opened it up on his lap. It had tomorrow's date on it. His eyes froze on the front page.

After several minutes of staring at that page, his lips began to move and something inside of him snapped.

Tears started to roll down his cheeks. He began to babble incoherently. Then, throughout the whole neighbourhood, a loud incessant wail broke through the quiet.

* * *

At seven o'clock the next morning, three workers stared in disbelief at the paper one of them held.

"I can't believe it," one of them said.

"Yeah, yesterday he ordered us to finish the demolition of this place today," the second man said. "Now the foreman has asked us to hold off on the job until the lawyers sort out his affairs."

The third man with the paper said he would check upstairs to ensure everything was secure before they left. As he passed the night table, he tossed the day's newspaper onto it, did a quick scan of the floor, and made his way downstairs to the others.

"A fantastic guy like that, and he was so rich. He must have been a financial genius," the first man said aloud, as the three of them left the building.

"Yeah, but to go like that," said the second man, as he locked the door of the old bookstore behind them.

On the front page of the newspaper on the night table was the headline "Local Millionaire Declared Insane". About thirty minutes later the paper faded away to yesterday.

942-472

I wrote this story with a pen in the 1960s and typed it into a computer in 2012. I modified it and edited it into its present form. Beware the children you adopt.

From the time they adopted Robert, he was strange. Susan and her husband John, noticed his head was bigger than normal. They had asked if he had any diseases or defects and the manager of the home showed them the record of his check-up. Some of the readings the doctor obtained were a little off but he certified him as healthy.

Somebody had left him on an orphanage's doorstep and Susan had to pick him up for a son. She and John thought it was a good idea at the time. They kept thinking about what an Einstein they would have but the dream ended quite quickly.

Robert grew up too fast for them. He was not normal in many ways. Although he grew up normally as far as size went, instead of playing with toys, he wanted to watch science programs on television, and after that, to read. She spent almost all her days in the library with him. She could not believe any person could read a book so fast, let alone a child.

By the time he was five, she almost hated him. When all the other children were out playing, he was reading science books. He had also started reading Shakespeare and could quote every word back. She continually lugged him to the library with lunch then stayed with him until the end of the day watching him read. She was not much of a reader.

Even his reading was weird as he just skimmed through each book, and could answer every question she asked him about its content. John soon became afraid the city library could not supply their son with all the books he asked for.

He read very little fiction, except for some of the classics and science fiction, which he found to be curiously funny with all the silly futuristic ideas they recounted. His main interests were science, engineering, and quite a lot of history. Soon, she was taking him to the university library to satisfy his hunger for more advanced material.

She could remember the first time he started to get on her nerves.

He had come from outside and she asked him, "Did you play baseball with the other boys, Robert?"

He responded rather callously, "No, why should I play with those simple-minded infants?"

She responded, startled, "You shouldn't speak that way about them."

"That's what they are. I get bored talking with them."

"It's not fair to say something like that about boys your age," she returned.

He glared at her and asked, "Is that all you can say about me?"

"Well, I'll be . . . You need to exercise and play with other boys," she said angrily. She could not believe his response.

"I realise I'm inside the library a lot but I also spend a lot of time roaming around the neighbourhood collecting insects and examining the plant life. I'd better leave now and go to my room to end this disagreeable encounter."

"Hold on, I'm not going to let you off that easily." She was getting very testy.

"Mother, I find that arguing is pointless in a situation as trivial as this."

She stood dumbfounded, as he left the kitchen and climbed the stairs to his room.

As soon as John came home, she told him what had happened and told him to do something about it.

He called Robert to come down.

"Do you wish anything, or do you wish to converse?" Robert asked when he arrived at the base of the stairs.

"We, ah . . . I just want to talk to you, son. We've been wondering why you're so different from the other kids. You're only five years old and you've never tried to enjoy yourself."

He replied, "Physical enjoyment is only for infantile people who can find nothing else to do with their time. Time is of grave importance. We do not exist for all eternity, you know. I enjoy learning."

"But you've taken the wrong approach with everyone around you. You can at least be more sensitive to your mother."

"No, you have the wrong approach. The argument is inconclusive and illogical with a closed mind. I certainly have no wish to argue with you or her."

John stood in shock at what Robert had said. They were in no mood for an argument. They could not sleep that night. Robert was not normal.

He grew up but did not change. He remained the same old Robert except he seemed to grow more powerful, such as one time when he was sitting at the kitchen table and John walked by. Robert asked out of nowhere, "What were you thinking about?"

John stuttered, "Whaa . . ." realising Robert was looking at him, expecting a reply.

Robert interrupted his father's thoughts. "You hate me, don't you? At least I have learned what that is. I can feel it. I can hear every thought that passes through your mind."

"What do you mean?"

"You had better change your attitude. You do not need to dislike me just because I am different from the other boys. You wish you had adopted someone more normal, do you not?"

"I think you're the one who should change your attitude with how you treat other children and adults. You belittle everyone."

"They are inferiors," he responded rather coldly.

"Cut that out. See, that's what you do all the time. You get me so angry when you do that."

"Anger and stupidity . . ." he said, to have the last word.

"One more crack out of you and I'll give you a spanking," John said in frustration.

"Such thoughts of violence . . ."

"I'll . . ."

John was going to smack him but he could not. He had the intention to but somehow Robert stopped him in mid-air. Robert did not move. John just could not move his arm.

"Such inferiors, . . . if I could be angry, I would have the right to act in your manner but conflict solves nothing."

If they hated him before, they loathed him now.

By the age of nine, he had finished high school, and he often mentioned the inferiority he saw in the teachers. Not one teacher liked him.

John realised that they had to do something, so they took Robert to a psychiatrist. They sat down with the psychiatrist afterwards.

He said, "I didn't get anywhere with him. He was using me for amusement, just someone to toy with. He ended up telling me what my problems were, and he was right on the mark. I gave him several intelligence tests and he flew through them. He is beyond any measure of genius we have."

At the age of ten, his parents decided to try to get him into a university. Many were interested but they did not want to take him, not because they thought he was not smart enough but because they had noticed he lacked maturity in social interactions.

His parents had a tough time but a university finally accepted him. They let him live in residence there. The same thing happened in grade school. He had all the professors baffled. They said he was very good in all the subjects. They could not teach him anything; he was always teaching and correcting them. They had an excellent physics program and they let him finish a four-year program in less than a year. Over the summer, he worked on a thesis.

There were a few noteworthy events in his short university stay though. One was when Robert was walking on campus and passed a small group of students.

A student named, Jim, condescendingly said to him, "Hi there, Shorty."

One of the girls in the group said, "Quit it, Jim, he's only about half your age."

"Then he should not be in university, Elizabeth," Jim responded.

"The kid's got brains," one of the boys said.

"He's only a kid, leave him alone," Elizabeth responded.

"I take it you are referring to me?" Robert stopped and interrupted the group's teasing.

"No, kid," said one of the other boys.

"Yeah, we are. I don't think I like the way you said that," said Jim.

"Leave the kid alone," said one of the other girls.

Robert never avoided a conflict so he said, "I do not wish to interrupt your childish prattle but I do not wish to hear such immaturity directed at me."

"You're asking for it, kid," Jim continued his mocking of Robert.

"Leave him alone," repeated Elizabeth.

"That kid must learn some cold facts," Jim continued aggressively.

"Cut it out, boys. Why don't you leave him alone? You're only jealous," Elizabeth continued.

"Oh, that's Elizabeth for you – always the goody-goody," Jim taunted her for her continuous nattering.

"Come on, let's go." Elizabeth pulled Jim's sleeve.

"I want to finish this first," was Jim's reply.

Jim pulled away from Elizabeth, quickly closed in on Robert and started to swing his fist at him but before his arm moved more than a few centimetres, he burst out in a scream of pain that knocked him unconscious and he slumped to the ground. Robert walked away with his nose in the air, as the rest of the group stood in mute surprise.

What had happened stunned Elizabeth and she was interested in getting to know more about this young man. She wanted to try to get him to notice her, even though she was much older than he was. She was one of the top students on campus and a rather dull girl, at least to the boys.

Finally, a few days after the incident, she spotted him in the cafeteria and approached him saying, "Hi, remember me? Would you help me with some physical chemistry exercises?"

This startled him and he said, "Why?" Then he thought a moment and reversed his decision. "I will do it because you were nice to me a few days ago. I do not have much time to spare, though, as I keep myself very busy."

"I'll take whatever time you can spare."

They smiled at each other.

She stated, "I'd like to apologise for Jim's behaviour the other day we met."

"Why? You did nothing wrong, so why apologise for his behaviour?"

"Well, that guy's a big jerk and a bully. Someone had to say or do something; but it looks as if you can look after yourself, although I don't know how you did what you did."

"I did not want him to strike me but I did not want to hurt him too much, just knock him out, as the gnat he is," Robert responded proudly.

"Why do you always talk that way? Do you hate everybody?"

"I cannot hate," he said brusquely.

"Well, you can sure make it seem that way," she said softly.

"You can take it any way you wish."

"Don't you love, or at least like, anyone?"

"I'm incapable of such trifles, although I think positively of the people who raised me, and to you who stood up for me but love – not really, unless you consider thinking positively a form of love."

"Love is not a trifle. You can't be human, if you can't love."

"Who says I'm human?"

That statement jolted her so much that she did not say another word.

He did help her with her studies several times. At one of those meetings, they got onto another topic.

"What do you believe in?" she asked him.

He looked at her, stunned, then answered, "You mean in a supreme being?" He read her mind. "You believe in nothing. I believe in facts."

"Don't you believe in God?"

"Belief without foundation is illogical. I know there is a God. It is a fact."

"Oh, you find God logical?" she quizzed.

"When your people get further along in their discoveries you'll find out. You search for a unifying theory but it is right in front of your face. I will not go further. You can find it yourselves."

"Is God linked to that?"

"I don't wish to discuss such trivialities. You will not understand."

"Well, what else can we talk about? I can't seem to talk to you about anything."

"Talking is an inefficient method of communication. I know what you think and how you feel. I know what you are going to say almost before you say it. Lower forms of life have to attach words for things they want to communicate then they have to mouth it through vocal cords and that makes communication very slow."

"Do you always have to speak as if people were ants and you're our god?"

"Well, am I not, in comparison?"

She did not remain his friend too much longer after that. She could not understand him at all. She thought he was too proud but as he told her, "I am incapable of such low forms of emotion."

He obtained his master's degree in physics and a doctorate in mathematics and astrophysics. At fifteen, he was overqualified but did get a job with a high-tech company in research.

At eighteen, he said to his parents at the kitchen table after a meal, "I wish to speak to you about several things. First, I find your people to contain one of the lowest forms of life in the universe. You run your lives on how you feel. Your emotions stifle your logic, if you have any. I may be leaving soon. I have studied your mannerisms, customs, language, and thoughts."

"What do you mean?" his mother asked.

"By our grading on your style of living, we would rate you a D minus. All you seem to be able to do well is fight. Conflict is almost a reflex action for your people and that's demonstrated collectively in your proclivity for war. You spend more money on implements of war than feeding your poor. Now, you're ready to push the button for the destruction of your planet for insignificant differences in ideologies. You attack other people when you do not even know them just because they are different in some way. I have experienced these types of things myself while living here."

She felt flabbergasted. "What's this 'our grading' you used? Isn't this your opinion, or are you a spy or something?"

"You only hear what you want to hear; you take what I say, ignore the meaning of it, and pick out the word 'our' but . . . I could say I was a spy, of a sort."

"A Russian spy?"

He met this question with such a look of amusement that they looked surprised he could show this "lowly" form of emotion.

He left them sitting, still in the kitchen, bemused as he went upstairs to his room. They were past the years of shock. Nothing he did or said shocked them anymore.

From his childhood, he had collected samples of insects, rocks, fossils, and just about anything else from tin cans to comic books.

Shortly after that outburst from him, he began packing up his collections.

One day his mother walked by his room as his door was open and asked him, "What are you doing?"

"What does it look like?" he replied rather brusquely.

"What are you doing with your collections?"

"At present, I'm packing them; later I'll be taking them with me."

"Taking them with you? Where?" she asked.

"Does it concern you?" he responded.

"Well, I'm your mother. Shouldn't I be told?"

"Mother only by adoption," he corrected.

"But I'm still your mother. I took care of you from the time you were a baby. Doesn't that count for something?"

There were a few moments of silence as he continued packing.

"Well, I'm not going to stop you from going," she said.

"You could not; I'm of age," he replied.

She had nothing left to say, so she left the room.

The next day, while he was out of the house, his mother went to his room, opened the door, and stared inside. He had already packed most of his things and hauled them out to the garage. He moved all the things he thought important there. He finally denuded the attic and basement of his entire . . . well at least she called it . . . junk. She snuck into his room, although she felt guilty about it. She rummaged through his drawers and found a book inside his desk. He kept this book as a type of diary but then again it was not. She started to read it. It seemed more like an entomology book, and they were the insects. He wrote down everything in it objectively as if he were observing them as one would study a disease germ. She skimmed through a few more of the pages and got so disgusted with the words he had used that she closed the book without going further. She placed it back into the drawer and closed it. It seemed to her a blessing to know he was leaving.

Then another question entered her mind. Where was he going? Was he leaving to get married or something? That thought made her laugh to herself but there was his encounter with that university friend of his – that girl.

"Well, guess who's here!" she suddenly heard behind her. Robert had returned.

She turned around but said nothing.

He stared back.

She knew he could read her thoughts. "You're the same old you, aren't you?" she finally said.

He gave no response.

"Well, say something," she said earnestly.

"There is nothing to say," he answered.

"You know, I've concluded you need more psychiatric help," she said firmly.

"Stupid humans," was all he said, shaking his head.

"No, honestly, you're living a dream. You're playing a role as if you're on a stage."

"Do not try to analyse a situation about which you know nothing."

"Look, it's like an alcoholic, if you don't admit you're ill, you can never be helped," she tried to reason with him.

"I find you fantastically amusing. You take bits of information and fly off in all directions but the correct one."

She gave him a disgusted sigh and left.

Two days later, he borrowed his parent's station wagon and began hauling his things away. When they asked where he was going, he said, "Somewhere in the country."

It took him a week to get it all out.

On the last day, she asked, "Are you keeping your stuff in someone's garage, or something?"

"No," he said.

"You're not keeping it out in the open, are you?" she asked.

"No, I would not do that. Why do my matters concern you so much?"

"Every parent cares about their children . . . Okay, do what you want to do. You're of age now. You probably have more brains than any other person on Earth."

"I have a brain capacity approximately three times that of an earthling," he announced.

"Oh, you figured it out!" she said, disgusted.

His last day was hectic. He only had one load left. In the morning, he took them in the station wagon to a car rental agency. After renting a car, John drove it back to their house with his wife in it. Robert arrived about a minute later in their station wagon.

Robert loaded the remaining items into the wagon and then came back into the kitchen where they had an early lunch.

When they finished, and had cleared the table, Robert pulled out a map and said, "At two o'clock leave to get to this location to pick up your car. This should get you to the site around three o'clock."

"Okay," said John as he took the map from Robert and looked at it carefully.

"You will be able to find it, will you?"

John replied, "Sure, it looks clear. We'll meet you there at three."

"Have you got everything?" she asked Robert.

"I do not forget anything," he said almost robotically.

Robert got up, went out the door, and left.

His parents sat at the table while John refolded the map. The full realisation of what was happening struck them. Their little boy had grown up and was about to leave. Everything he had was gone. They were puzzled, though. They had thought he was going to another university, or maybe to a new job but the dot on the map was not in any city but a spot in the middle of nowhere in the countryside. Was he moving to a quiet reclusive spot in the country to live, or maybe rent a place for a while?

They reminisced about their life with him. It had been anything but boring and was quite unexpected; he was a unique individual. Maybe they had been too harsh with him and had overreacted to him because he was so different. Before, she had thought that she would feel as if this was a good-riddance event but it was hard, no matter how strange he may be, not to become attached to him.

Two o'clock came quickly. It was time to go and pick up the station wagon. They had offered to give him their car, as they were thinking of getting a new one anyway. It would have been a nice send-off gift for him but he had said he did not need it.

As he said, they arrived near the spot around three but there was nothing there. They looked at the map again and realised the location was off the highway on a small roadway, so they pulled off the highway and followed a mud path about one and a half kilometres into a heavily wooded area until they reached an old abandoned farmhouse. They parked their station wagon beside it.

Robert must have heard the rented car arrive, as he came right out of the house.

"Hi, you two," he called out.

They got out of the car and went toward him. They thought he was going to lead them into the house, or just say goodbye right where they were; instead, he started walking down a less travelled continuation of the mud road until they reached the edge of a forest. He walked several metres into it until they came to a clearing, only it was not very clear. In the middle of it was a wide cylindrical object, about twenty-five metres in diameter.

Robert continued heading toward the object until he was almost beside it. He turned around, smiled at them, and said, "Do not be afraid. I can sense your fear but there is nothing to be afraid of. It's time for me to go soon and I called my ship back to Earth. I have seen enough."

They had stopped two steps from him.

"Are we going to pick up the cars now?" John asked nervously.

Robert responded, "If you want to but you're welcome to spend some time with me; after all, as you say, you are my parents. I have spent my life living at your home; you can stay with me awhile."

John asked, "Are we going to the house?"

"No, it's quite rotten and unsafe. No one had used it in many years. I can show you my place, or at least my place until I get back to my planet," said Robert softly.

John looked at Susan for several seconds. They were not sure if they wanted to visit his place.

"Do not come, if you feel uncomfortable," Robert said. "I can walk you to the cars and you can leave."

She was not sure if she wanted to leave. If this was true, she was curious about what this shiny thing was.

She looked at her husband and said, "I'd like to go, John. This looks interesting. Maybe Robert would like to show us his place."

"Yes, come on, Dad," Robert repeated. "I stayed at your place, so you can at least see mine."

"How can this be yours, if you've lived with us all these years? How did you know this even existed?" John asked.

"Very good question; how about let us sit down inside and I'll tell you all about it. I promise you we will not go anywhere."

She was eager but John was not. He was not the adventurous type. He liked to have his feet firmly planted on the ground. She poked him a few times and he suppressed his thoughts of claustrophobia and took a couple of steps toward the cylinder. Robert then led them to the open staircase to the insides of the ship. He reached back, took her hand, and led her inside with John following reluctantly behind.

It was very bright inside. It looked a little larger from the inside than the outside. Everywhere there were blinking lights. Every square centimetre seemed to have a purpose.

Robert made a hand motion by one part of a wall and a foldout cot slid out, then a plastic cover slid on top. "Here's my bed," he said. "The plastic air-sealed dome is in case the craft gets punctured while I'm asleep."

He waved his hand over the centre of the room and a table with two chairs slowly rose from the centre of the floor. "Unfortunately, this craft can hold a maximum of two people but please sit on the chairs. I can sit on the cot," he said proudly.

They sat down. He brought them two glasses of some beverage and two objects on a plate that looked much like éclairs. She tasted one of the éclairs and it was delicious, like a sweet fruit flavour. She sipped the beverage and it had a strange taste. She thought it was supposed to be a type of tea but it was a little too tart for her taste. He sat on the cot and then proceeded to answer all their questions without their asking.

"First, let me apologise for my unpleasant demeanour most times. I have been very frustrated with the progress of you earthlings. I do not want to leave you with a sour taste in your mouth.

"Let me inform you first about me. I arrived on your planet as an infant, so I would grow up among your people and develop an identity here on Earth. My government implanted in my brain what would eventually become my knowledge of who I was and what I was to do. They camouflaged this ship and left it behind on the other side of the moon until I was ready to leave.

"As you know, I do have a form of telepathy, so I can read your minds, and it allowed me a means to communicate with this ship when I was ready to leave. This, as you have determined, is my spaceship to get me to my home planet. I guess it's hard to call it home. I grew up on your planet but I was 'born' somewhere else. I am anxious to get back to my home. I do not remember seeing it at all. All I know is your planet, and I will keep memories from here as long as I live.

"What I have found here is humans have indeed advanced from the last time we were here but mostly technologically. You have done a pretty good job of controlling science but you have advanced so slightly psychologically and socially. You are sociopaths; unable to live with each other in peace, from how you live together as mates, to how you interact as nations. Your people cannot get past your selfish greed. You endlessly compete for more things, more territory, more of everything. You have people on your planet who starve while others grow fat. You have nations who create and amass huge stockpiles of armaments and sell them to others to kill each other.

"What kind of world is this? You grew in population through advances in medicine and grew in knowledge in science and technology. However, you have dictators who rule greedily over countries by force of will to serve themselves. You also have leaders of democracies that rule countries by pandering to the greed of the masses without consideration of the cost. Either way, you are on the road to the destruction of your world. You drain all the limited resources of your planet not for peace and exploration of your universe but for immediate self-gratification. I fear, that when my people visit your planet in the future, it will be dead. If so, we can leave your planet for the colonisation by others.

"As I said, we have been here before but what have you done with the guidance we have imparted? To the Greeks, we sent several people to try to influence them in the right direction but they turned them into mythical gods. The Norse did the same thing. We have sent others in different eras and parts of the world. Always you take our words and twist them to your purposes.

"Am I bitter? Yes. I had thought maybe I could stay here longer and impart some wisdom to your leaders but I do not think it will make any difference. I'm leaving you to your own devices." He sighed.

"I guess I had better go, now. I have said enough. I have taken my collection in my ship as mementoes of my trip. My people will place them in the Museum of Earth on my planet. Despite how I acted, I leave here with fond thoughts of you and I have appreciated your putting up with me all these years."

He stood up, held out his hand to his parents, shook their hands, and gave them each a warm hug. He walked them to their cars and smiled at them but somehow it looked like a sad smile.

His mother said, "Don't be so sad. I hope we surprise the next person who comes and we'll still be here."

He replied, "I hope so, too."

"Do you have another name or can we still call you Robert?" she asked.

There was a slight hesitation.

"There seems to be no logical reason why I should not tell you – it's 942-472."

"942-472; your planet gives you a number!" she said incredulously.

"Yes, the 942 is your planet's number and the 472 is the number given to me as the 472nd person to visit your planet."

"Even your name is logical," John grunted.

"Well, then goodbye, Robert . . . 942-472," she said, as they exchanged hugs for the last time. She had tears in her eyes. She realised this young man was maybe not such a bad person. He was just different from them.

He gave them these final words.

"You will not see anything when I leave. After I get inside, I will activate the ship's cloaking system. Your people will not see me on your radar. We did not have to do it much in the past but your technology of detection is much better now. Your people tried to kill the last person to visit you. He managed to feign death so he could escape. 942-471, or Jesus, as they called him, also ended up deified. His adoptive parents, Joseph, and Mary, got the right message but his followers misrepresented him to others. You are an odd people." He stood quietly for a minute.

He shook his head disappointedly, turned, and walked back up the path to his spaceship.

His parents remained for a time, staring at the brush behind the farmhouse. They saw nothing but there was an odd wind that arose shortly after he left and entered the trees.

Many years after Robert had left, his mother told her pastor about her son. "What do think, Pastor?"

"My God," he said incredulously, "you've experienced the Second Coming of Christ. Armageddon may be coming. He,

Robert the Christ, has told you the Truth of what is to come. If man does not repent of his ways, destruction will come to this Earth. You two are the father and mother of He who will rule the world in the after-days. I must teach others about this New Testament.

ALTERED LIFE

This is another story, written by pen in the 1960s, transcribed by typewriter, then to computer much later in the 1990s, maturing as it went. This is a story of a young couple trying to start their new lives while running into bumps along the way; some bumps more unusual than others.

Mary Boules was a slim and good-looking young woman despite the hardship of the last couple of years. Her long auburn hair glistened in the sun like jewels. Her intense blue eyes were like wells into the depths of her soul. She was a quiet person with a very positive disposition. Her husband, Norman, thought the world of her.

Norman Boules was of average build and had dashing red hair and dark blue eyes, "like the ocean", Mary would say. He was a pensive person but did not do well in school. He was more inclined to be the life of every party, the fool in every class.

Mary met Norman in elementary school and they moved from being childhood friends to high school sweethearts. They were too in love to get an education beyond school.

They wanted to get married and start their life together. They had a simple wedding and no honeymoon. Mary landed a job as a clerk in the local grocery store. Norman was fortunate to get a job in the construction industry as an apprentice painter.

As soon as he got his job, they bought a small bungalow on a quiet street. Within six months, Mary was pregnant and seven months later she quit her job to finish her pregnancy and become a full-time mother. They had a beautiful little boy, Norman Junior, who immediately became the centre of their lives. Their finances were tight with only one salary, and with the addition of a new member to the family, they were barely keeping up with their payments.

About twelve months later, his company laid him off due to a slowdown in house construction. Government employment insurance, welfare, and odd jobs were not enough to keep them afloat and they began to fall behind in their mortgage payments. Finally, the housing industry improved and his boss hired him again.

Despite that good news, the interest on their debt held them in a debt spiral. Norman could not afford to upgrade his skills, nor could they pull out of the tailspin. Moreover, even if Mary went back to work, she would not make enough to pay for daycare for their son. Their initial optimism for their marriage was waning.

Despite their problems, Mary had promised herself that today would be a cheery one and spent a pleasant day with Junior. That evening, she looked at her watch and then glanced out the kitchen window in anticipation of her husband's arrival. She returned to her task of finishing making supper. When she heard the familiar sound of her husband's car pulling into the driveway, she rushed to the front door of the house. She could hear the car door slam shut.

She opened the door, smiling. Norman had had a busy day on the job but despite it, he smiled back and leaned forward to give her a little kiss. "Any mail?" he asked.

"Yes," she responded.

He settled into his ripped-up old easy chair in their small living room. One glance through the mail disclosed his creditors had not given up on him. His look became graver as he sat perusing bill after bill. Mary recognised his mood and left him so she could finish making supper. It did not take her long and, within ten minutes, Norman got up in answer to her summons to the supper table. They ate in silence. Norman amused himself by feeding the toddler and later playing with him before pulling him from the highchair.

Mary got up to clear the table and Norman put the child into his playpen so he could help Mary do the dishes. Later, Norman played with Junior until it was time to put him to bed, and then they settled into their chairs in the living room.

"All I could see in the mail today were bills," he opened.

"Our credit cards are maxed out. I can't use them anymore," she added.

"Well, I pay them as much as I can each month. With all the bills we get, how in the world can I hope to pay a large amount to any one creditor?" He said exasperatedly, "We can't even do what we used to do by paying off one bill with a loan from another creditor. If we don't solve our problem soon, we'll be bankrupt.

"I phoned a credit counsellor during morning break, as we discussed earlier. He said he could see us Saturday." He sat pensively for a minute then continued, "I was hoping we could have a nice home together and we could build a family. Now we'll have to delay that idea. The housing market seems to be picking up, and I hope I can hold onto this new job. I'm trying to impress the boss as best I can. Unfortunately, even if both of us work now, we won't make enough to pull us out of this hole. Maybe we will have to sell our house – or the bank's house – or go on welfare but if we go there, we may not be able to work at all, so we'll never get off welfare."

"You don't think we'd have to do any of that, do you?"

"Maybe but let's leave that until Saturday. Perhaps the counsellor will help us make some decisions."

They could see the sun was setting and Junior was asleep, so they moved to the old wooden rocker out in their backyard and watched the sunset become a black starry sky.

The blackness awed Mary. "It's so clear tonight. The stars look so bright," she said excitedly.

"The moon isn't up yet. It's beautiful, isn't it? It gets my mind off my troubles. It makes me feel so small."

"Remember when we were young and the hours that we spent trying to count the stars?"

"Yeah, kind of dumb, wasn't it?"

"Why do you say that?"

"I don't know. There are so many of them and many aren't stars, they're galaxies."

"We fell in love under these stars." Mary paused. "Do you still love me, Norman?"

He turned his head toward her. "What are you talking about? Of course, I love you. 'Until death do us part', right? We're not going to let anything ruin that. Our love is forever. I mean it. Don't you ever forget that?"

She snuggled close to him and put her head on his shoulder. He looked at her and could see she was crying.

"Now don't start with the sob stuff. Every time I say I love you; you do your sob thing." He put his arm around her. Her sentimentality was one of the traits he loved about her. Time passed. Norman checked his watch. "We'd better get to bed; it's getting late."

In the morning, Mary rose noiselessly and went to the kitchen to start breakfast, leaving her husband to sleep awhile longer. She heard Junior rustling in his bed and quietly picked him up, strapped him into his high chair and gave him a small container of dried cereal to keep him amused for a while.

Norman was waking up himself when he heard a loud call from his wife, "Norman?"

He tossed in bed, startled. What is the matter? I do not get up this early, he thought as he looked at the mechanical alarm clock, and turned the alarm mechanism off. He called out, "What's the matter, Mary?"

"The stove isn't working," she answered. "I turned it on a few minutes ago, and the element isn't hot yet. I've never had this happen before."

"Is the clock on it working?"

There was a pause, and she responded, "No, and when I opened the oven door, the light didn't go on."

"Okay. Maybe it's broken or the circuit breaker has popped. Meanwhile, plug in the kettle and make some toast. We can at least have that for breakfast. I'll be out in a minute."

"But the kettle doesn't work either and the toaster too. I opened the fridge and the light didn't go on."

Norman was frustrated, now. He got out of bed, grabbed a flashlight from the night table, and ventured down into the basement. He examined the breakers but everything looked fine.

He returned upstairs. "It's hard to believe the power is out. I don't think the electric company would just cut us off. It might be a power failure."

He reached over and picked up the telephone book. With a quick search, he found the number for the company, picked up the receiver and began punching the numbers. Halfway through he noticed the lack of a tone when he pressed the buttons. He hung up, picked it up again, and put it to his ear. There was no sound coming through the receiver. He pressed a couple of numbers again. There was still no sound – no ringing, no answering, nothing.

Things were very strange. It was rare the power and telephone were out of commission at the same time.

Mary went over to the counter and picked up her cell phone. "Here, try this." She handed it to him.

He looked at it and noted it was not picking up a signal. All of this was getting to be too much for him. What else could go wrong? He resolved that, as soon as he could dress and leave the house, he was going to get to a pay phone. He was just about to head back to the bedroom to dress when his wife mentioned she had flushed the toilet while he was in the basement, and there was no water filling the tank. She remarked that all the utility companies must have cut them off.

Norman reminded her that utilities usually warned people before that happened. It was also highly unlikely all the utility companies would cancel a customer on the same day.

He told her to forget about making breakfast for him because he could grab a bite to eat on the way to work. He knew, that if he did not hurry, he would not be able to make his telephone calls at a booth early enough to avoid being late for work.

He turned and went to the bedroom to dress. He had just begun to put on his pants when he heard a blood-curdling scream from the front of the house. He struggled to dress while he raced out of the bedroom. Suddenly, he stopped short. His hands released his pants, letting them fall to the floor. Mary had pulled open the curtains and was standing in front of the window shocked and shaking at the sight before her. The loud noise from her scream had started Junior crying.

Norman stared at what he saw in disbelief. Perhaps this was a prank but how, why? He finally regained his senses, and curiosity forced him to go to the front door, open it, and go outside. If this was a prank, it sure looked authentic but he knew it could not be. Nobody could put together a prank as complex as this was. He glanced back at Mary. She had wandered to the door beside him and stood gaping as her eyes surveyed the scene before her.

He stepped farther outside the house to look around and Mary followed.

"This has to be a nightmare!" Norman said aloud. He reached over and gave his arm a little pinch but the view remained.

"Would you believe last night I prayed to God to help us?" Mary said incredulously.

"You've never done that before but I don't think this is the help you expected."

Mary began to cry silently. What she had seen overwhelmed her. She turned to go back inside the house where it seemed more real.

Over the past few months, Norman's self-esteem had ebbed with his inability to financially support his family but now, he was not sure if he had any control at all in his life. They both had friends, family, and other support to help them in their trials. Now, he wondered whether they could survive this without them.

Norman turned, entered the house, and looked down beside the door at his bag of painting clothes, shoes, and lunchbox that Mary had filled for him earlier in the morning in readiness for his day at work. He glanced over at Mary who was now in the kitchen caressing their son in her arms while walking and comforting him. This was all he had now. This was his world. He closed the door.

He went over to Mary and baby Norman and gave them a huge hug while tears formed in his eyes. He left them after a few minutes and plopped down in his old chair to try to make sense of what was outside.

Gone were the street, the other houses, and the rest of their neighbourhood. Gone was his car. What remained of his yard was part of his driveway and grass which looked as if something had cut it into a circle big enough to contain the house and basement dropped into a huge sphere.

In the remainder of the sphere, was a menagerie of different plants cut and dropped as his house had been. The sphere must have had an Earth-like gravity around its entire inner surface to hold all the plants in place around his house and above their heads. He spotted several areas with large pools of water, probably ponds for aquatic plants and animals. He turned his head and saw a robin, appearing somewhat disoriented, flitting from one tree to another. Norman guessed that, even if he had not spotted an animal, there must have been some hidden and perhaps as disoriented as he was within this collection.

In the 'sky' in the centre of the sphere he spotted a huge central ball of light illuminating the entire space. He had seen thin strands of support wires with tiny nozzle-like appendages on them leading from the sphere to the ball. He guessed they were for a watering system. He saw two larger cables he suspected were the power supply for the giant light.

He knew his life would never be the same again.

* * *

Grogney and Schleft looked at the control panel in front of them.

"We're almost outside of this solar system," Grogney said.

"Good, now we can soon slip into hyper-drive and speed on home," Schleft responded.

"The last time our people were here, it wasn't so hard to get around. This time we had to cloak ourselves almost the entire time. It uses up a tremendous amount of power. The dominant species have advanced quite dramatically."

"Yeah, I noticed. Now they have radar, infrared and other forms of detection they did not have before. They might have advanced but it isn't in the areas they should have. What a waste of technology."

"It's been more than 1000 years since our people were last here."

"It'll be interesting to study the changes in their flora and fauna since then. I suspect we're going to see a big drop in the diversity of species."

"The dominant species are still very barbaric, aren't they; still interested in killing each other while destroying their environment."

"Yes, over the thousands of years we've been visiting them, that is the one thing that hasn't changed significantly. Their technology has advanced far beyond their capability to handle it."

"I'm afraid they will cause their extinction, and probably that of all the other creatures on that planet."

"Well, let our scientists determine that. If it's found by their experiments using a risk model that these creatures will likely destroy the other life forms on the planet, they will have to decide whether we return here soon to eliminate them so they do not turn their planet into a wasteland."

"Yes, and these two specimens we picked up will become the determinants of whether the other members of their species will be spared or not. This planet is so unlucky. Each time we wiped out a species of violent bipeds with hopes another one would be better; the next evolved contender ended up as bad as, or worse than, the previous one. This time though, there is no current other contender. In the past, we had Australopithecus, habilis, erectus, neanderthalensis, etc. and one after the other we had to eliminate them. If another intelligent biped is to take over now, they will have to evolve again from the apes."

"I hope the people we've chosen are a good representation of their species because the fate of the existence of their species rests on what we find out about them."

IO

This is another old story from the 1960s, about a geologist who tries a little too hard to get rich. When I originally wrote it, it was only about half the length and I called it "Eureka". I kept the basic idea of the story but I revamped it to make it more current.

System Exploration and Mining Inc., or SEM, was a huge mining conglomerate that scoured the solar system looking for valuable ores, minerals, and gems in enough quantity for profitable mining. Its geologists had explored Mars and Venus and found no profitable ore there. The Asteroids were where they made their fortune, and now they were planning to search the moons of Jupiter.

For the journey, the company constructed a huge specially-built ship to launch from a base in Earth orbit. It even had a hydroponics centre to grow plants to replenish the oxygen, reduce carbon dioxide, and provide food for the crew.

When they found gold and other precious metals, the crew loaded the ship with the treasure and jettisoned waste materials, excess supplies, equipment, and empty fuel bladders.

The ship carried a crew of seven consisting of a captain, an engineer, a helmsman, a communications officer, a cook, a physician, and a geologist. It also had three scientists who would research Jupiter and its satellites. Universities had paid a lot of money to have them make the trip with their instruments into this unexplored area of the solar system. Fred Dory was the geologist on board. He had twelve years of experience and a knack for choosing mining sites. He had brought immense wealth to the firm, and the company rewarded him well for his work, including giving him the honour of being the first geologist to visit the moons of Jupiter.

The management selected the crew for their capabilities in their respective primary functions aboard the ship, and for their backup capabilities in case something happened to any other members of the crew. For example, the captain was a very capable engineer.

SEM built the ship in two sections: the rear end was principally for storing food, fuel, and supplies but would store ore when they reached Jupiter. The front end was much smaller and could detach for use as a vessel to land on the moons. The lander stored two exploration vehicles: The Pathfinder and the Explorer.

The managers equipped the ship with a space sail which would use the solar wind to continue to accelerate the ship toward Jupiter to help conserve fuel. The Sun's gravity would play that role on the way back. The crew would use the space sail again to decelerate the ship on its return to Earth.

There was much fanfare when the ship finally blasted its rockets to start its mission to Jupiter. It was a long journey from Earth – over a year and a half each way and one year of mining and exploring. No manned flights had gone that far before.

The trip to Jupiter was uneventful and boring. For amusement, the crew played games, read, watched movies, listened to music, and engaged in physical activities to keep in shape. To help maintain muscle tone and keep bone density, the ship produced an artificial gravity close to that of Earth.

To keep their psychological equilibrium, they had frequent communication with their families on Earth. At first, communication was two-way normal video but as the distance between speakers increased the lag, even with the message sent at the speed of light, became so long it got awkward and they switched to sending video packages.

Three months into the trip Fred got a message from his wife, Joan, that shocked him. First, it had started with small talk, mostly about family, friends, and neighbours, and from his side, life on the ship.

Suddenly, Joan changed her tone. "I've got some other news," she said ecstatically.

"Oh, about Mom or Dad?"

"No, more about us." She hesitated. "I've known for a few weeks but wanted to make sure."

Fred was a bit puzzled. "What do you mean?"

"You're going to be a father."

"What?" he raised his voice in shock.

"Aren't you happy?"

He was too stunned to answer.

"Well, why the big silence? It sounds as if you're not happy or something," she broke the quiet.

"You shouldn't have gotten pregnant before I left."

"Why not?"

"Because you knew I was going away. Heck, we just got married a few days before I left. I didn't want to do that. I wanted to wait until I got back."

"I wanted you to have something to look forward to. Aren't you happy?"

"Right now, it's more of a mixed reaction. I don't know what to say. You put me on the spot. You're going to have a baby and I won't be there. We didn't discuss that. You're rushing things. You know I love kids, and I want to experience their lives. I want to be there for them. I'll be millions of kilometres away."

"But we'll talk every day and sometimes more, so it's as if you're here," she said excitedly. "Think of me, I'll have a little part of you here with me. It'll keep me company and it'll always remind me of you."

"But I won't experience that. I love you so much, Joan. Just thinking of you makes me pine to get back and it's distracting. Now a baby will make it worse."

"I'm sorry then," she responded disappointedly.

"Don't be sorry. It's done. I'll get over it. Just focus on keeping yourself healthy. Remember always that I love you but I can't say I'll be back soon. I still have about four years to go. We're not even at Mars yet . . . I'd better get back to work."

"Do you want to know what it is?" she asked before he cut her off.

"Do you know?"

"Not yet, I'll leave that up to you."

"Let's leave it as a surprise then, unless you feel strongly that you'd like to know."

"No, it's okay."

"It's about time to go. I love you."

"I love you too, Fred. Keep safe."

"I'll call you later in the day."

They exchanged air kisses and closed off the conversation.

When he spread the news to the other crew members, they were all delighted to hear it. For dinner, they had a little celebration.

Six months later, he got a message from his wife in the hospital. She had delivered a little boy. They named him Marshal in honour of Fred's father.

When they finally neared Jupiter, its size awed them. Seeing it from Earth as a speck of dust in the sky or as an object in a telescope was no match for the beauty found in that magnificent planet up close. If they wandered too close to the planet its gravity would not let them escape.

Their job was to scan for ore on the four large moons and more than fifty-nine smaller moons orbiting Jupiter. The crew would scan most of the small moons and moonlets first as they were farther from the planet and because their asteroid-like size may contain some of the wealth found among the asteroid belt. They then would scan the large moons but what they knew from unmanned flybys, it was unlikely they would find profitable ore on them. There was no plan to examine the small Jovian inner moons as they were too close to Jupiter.

As the spaceship approached the outermost moonlets, the crew began their scan and, instead of travelling in the orbital plane of the moons, they travelled above it to reduce the odds of the ship being damaged by the myriads of small particles which could puncture it, because of their high relative velocities.

At first, they had no luck, until a small rock that passed by them tested positive. Their eyes lit up. When another rock tested positive, they rolled out the Pathfinder, which had various attachments to mount on the front of it. Normally on a moon, they would use either the front scoop (for loading ore) or a V front (for pushing through boulders and stones) but for trapping small objects in space it had a box-type front end with a funnel in front of it to direct the rocks into it.

The engineer fastened the box onto the Pathfinder, and the helmsman got into his space suit and entered the small vehicle. The engineer evacuated the air from the storage area and opened the outer door. The helmsman then fired the vehicle's rockets to propel it out into space.

Fred soon got another promising reading. The helmsman manoeuvred the Pathfinder near the rock, matched its velocity, and opened the door to the box. He accelerated the vehicle slightly so the rock entered the interior.

When the box was full, they brought the little vehicle back into the ship and dumped the contents of the box into the cargo hold. While the Pathfinder was out collecting more, the crew processed the ore and discarded the worthless rock back into orbit around Jupiter.

They were extremely pleased the ore quality was high. When the number of ore-bearing rocks increased, they brought the Explorer into service and the collection process proceeded in earnest twenty-four hours a day.

During this time, the researchers spent a lot of time scanning the environment around Jupiter, including its magnetic field and its influence on the surrounding satellites, both large and small.

About six months later, the team used the Pathfinder for research purposes with one of the scientists in his space suit inside it manoeuvring a large block of frozen waste material into place to send it on a trajectory toward Jupiter. Inside the block were instruments to measure the composition of the atmosphere and collect pressure, temperature, and wind velocity data. Suddenly, a fast-moving rock orbiting the planet smashed through the Pathfinder.

Fred, in the Explorer, was gathering ore at the time. He sped over to the Pathfinder and quickly released the block of probes to send it on its way to Jupiter. He then hooked up to the Pathfinder and sped over to the spaceship and into the airlock. When the team opened the Pathfinder, they found it badly damaged and the scientist was dead. The rock had pierced his suit and let the air out. He had died almost instantly. The Pathfinder was unrepairable. They kept it for spare parts in case something happened to the Explorer.

Using only one vehicle slowed the ore collection process but the number of nuggets found was dropping off as they got closer to Jupiter. Weeks went by as they continued to pull in the ore. Slowly they filled most of the cargo area of the ship.

They had gotten close to Calisto, Jupiter's most distant and second-largest moon, about the same size as Mercury. The scientists were studying its cratered surface, which looked a lot like Earth's moon, to check if it had a large quantity of water just beneath its surface. Preliminary results indicated that it did. They pulled in the Explorer and ceased mining.

The ship fired a blast and manoeuvred into orbit around Calisto. The crew sent off an unmanned probe to land on its surface to study it further while other sensors searched for any signs of minable ore but there was none. The precious metal in it was randomly dispersed throughout the moon.

For a week, they circled so they could further their studies with radar and other equipment to discover all they could about it. They learned that the crust on the surface was strong enough for ships to land on it, and for the construction of a future base.

When they finished, they broke orbit and moved on to Ganymede, the next innermost and largest moon in the solar system. They found it much like Calisto in composition but only a part of it had cratered; the rest of it was darker and smoother. Their studies revealed it had tectonic plates like Earth and the dark area was smooth lava.

Europa was next. It was the fourth largest moon, slightly smaller than Earth's moon, and distinguished itself by its smooth surface filled with streaks and cracks, which they confirmed was due to the large amount of ice on its surface. Again, the scientists probed its surface with all the equipment they had, including surface probes.

The scientists sent another type of probe which would pick up and return a sizable sample of ice to analyse for carbon compounds – indicators of life but they found no evidence of it.

Another week later, they reached Io; a moon unlike any other in the solar system, with over four hundred active volcanoes, high radiation levels, and an electrical charge, all due to its proximity to Jupiter. It was the third-largest moon.

Because of the strength of Jupiter's gravitational field, they decided to establish their orbit around Io parallel to the surface of the giant planet.

Even before they reached Io, Fred was getting some interesting readings on its surface. The crew manoeuvred into a stable orbit around it.

"Wow, I get great readings on this moon," Fred said excitedly.

"Finally found something interesting, huh?" responded the captain. "We won't be able to take much time to look at it though; we've almost run out of time. We won't be able to pick up much ore from Io but it'll be good to know for future operations."

The captain looked at Fred and commented, "I heard you sent another message out to your wife earlier today."

"Yes."

"How is everything at home?"

"Great, Marshal is growing like a weed and getting into lots of mischief, as I did when I was a kid."

The rest of the crew chuckled.

"I sure wish I was there." Fred added, "I'm missing his growing up."

"You send messages to them once or twice a day."

"That's different from being there. I'd love to cuddle him and play with him."

"I can understand that. There are three other people on board in similar situations."

"But their kids are older and they already have spent time with them."

"When we get back, you can catch up. He'll still be young; he'll only be four. I know you have retired. You were the one who took SEM's offer to go to Jupiter. You could have waited until you got back to get married."

"Marrying was Joan's idea. That was her promise to be faithful until I came back but I didn't know she'd get pregnant. That wasn't part of the deal."

"Maybe it was a gift for you on your arrival. I imagine you'll go back into retirement when you return."

"Dammed right, I'll be gone for good when this trip ends. I already had enough money to live comfortably. With this trip, I'll be filthy rich. Pretty well everything I have is in SEM stocks, and when we arrive with this load, the stock is going to shoot up to the sky. Too bad we couldn't get a little bit more ore. We still have some space for more."

"Don't get greedy. To be safe, we should be leaving for Earth soon. With the money I'll get, I may just retire myself."

There were a few nods from the rest of the crew with that comment.

The crew worked in silence as the scan continued. The scientists ran their scans of Io. They sent two more cubes of waste material filled with probes into Jupiter. The engineer spent his time ensuring the lander and Explorer was ready to descend to Io's surface. They took turns having naps.

After almost two days, Fred's scan was finished and he analysed the results. "Wow, it looks as if there are two very promising ore beds on Io. Can we get down on the surface and see what we have? I'd like to verify the results. Is there any way we can top up the ship with any ore we find?"

"Sorry, as I said earlier, we've got to get out of here soon or we'll miss our window to get back. Our voyage home will get longer as we stay here plus, we lost the Pathfinder so we wouldn't be able to collect much anyway," the captain responded.

"Okay, why take the chance. Let's find a landing spot near site one, if possible, then we can get out of here. That lode looks very promising indeed."

The surface of Io was extremely hot, rocky, and marred by many crevasses and old lava beds. Its volcanoes regularly spewed sulphur and lava. It was particularly subject to quakes due to its proximity to Jupiter. After a careful review of the surface scan data, they found a suitable place to land but it was going to be tricky because of the small space available. Although the site was relatively far from the ore beds, it was the closest suitable site to both and was closer to site two. The best feature was the beds were on Io's bright side. As Earth's moon, the same half of Io always faces its planet.

"What's your opinion on the stability of Io?" the captain enquired.

"Not very good," Fred responded. "That's going to be a factor in the decision on mine-ability. The information I've got so far is these ore beds seem quite close to the surface, so mining will be relatively easy. Quakes can be tough to predict but my guess is Io should be stable long enough for us to look at what it has. We should be okay at least until nineteen hundred hours."

"Okay," the captain said, "the helmsman will set the lander down on that landing site and will wait for you until nineteen hundred hours maximum. I don't want to take any chances. You're good at predicting these sorts of things. You're sure you'll have enough time to do everything?"

"I calculated the distances to each site, my speed, and the type of ground I'll cover. I should have lots of time to spare," Fred said confidently.

The helmsman, communications officer, and Fred got into their spacesuits and boarded the lander. Once the three of them settled in, the lander separated from the ship and rocketed down to Io's surface.

When the crew finally landed, Fred was so enthusiastic that he was the first one to unsnap his harness. He exited the airlock of the lander, while the two remaining crew members unlocked and opened the cargo bay from inside then lowered the Explorer to the ground. Fred entered the vehicle that would be his home while he manoeuvred across Io. He had nineteen hours to explore the two sites and stake his claims.

With its "V" blade pushing aside most of the rocks and boulders, the Explorer struggled to site two. There, Fred found a very rich ore bed. An intense scan of the site showed it would be worth sending a ship to mine it but by itself, it would be only marginally profitable. The yield looked very good, mostly of copper, silver, and gold. Fred prepared a claim stake and fired it out of the vehicle to embed it into the site. The stake had a radio transmitter that would inform other vessels arriving near Io that they had a lawful claim on its geological treasures. No one else could make any claims, nor take any wealth from here, under penalty of the law.

Fred had a decision to make now: He could forget visiting the other site, or go there with the hopes it was as good as, or better than, this site. The ground was going to be rough to travel though. He looked at his chronometer, made a mental calculation, and decided to go for it.

It was an extremely rough ride. When he arrived at site one, all he could do was gape. This was the largest seam he had ever seen. He glanced at his chronometer. He had made good time but the ground's surface was rougher than he thought and he did not have a comfortable margin of error for getting back to the lander; however, he just had to see this. All he could think of was, 'Ten per cent of this is mine'.

He climbed out onto the surface and could see the readings on his radiation monitor jumping around erratically. Around him was rocky waste but even a novice geologist could see a multi-billion-dollar seam of gold, platinum, palladium, and silver laid at his feet. He did a thorough close scan of the site to confirm his observations. The lode was almost pure metal so refining it would be relatively easy and it was almost all near the surface, which made it easier and safer to mine. He picked up a chunk and caressed it in his gloved hands. He would take this as a memento of the find. This chunk alone would be worth several hundred thousand dollars.

He was about to pick up more ore for the rest of the crew when a call thundered in his helmet from the Explorer's computer voice. "Must return to the lander. The landing site is nine hours away. The time now is ten hundred and ten hours. Ship leaving nineteen hundred hours. Must allow for the terrain. Delay has made it necessary to make a new faster schedule. Return immediately."

Fred had learned never to argue with a computer. He rushed into the Explorer, got inside, and filed his claim on the recorder.

Again, the speaker boomed, "Must leave immediately. Lander leaves at nineteen hundred hours. Cannot be delayed. Radioactivity level rising and increased quake activity detected."

Fred settled into his seat, prepared a claim stake, and fired it out of the vehicle to embed it into the site. He jumped to the controls, set the small craft to autopilot, and let the computer do the rest. It would compute the fastest route to take. He felt the jerk as the Explorer quickly began the trek back to the lander. Fred fastened his harness and hoped for the best. He was certain he would get back safely. He transmitted the information about the sites to the ship so it could register its claim officially.

Almost five hours into the trip, the speaker cut in on his thoughts. "Radio contact lost. Unable to reconnect. Quake activity substantially increasing. Warning!"

Fred checked the communicator and noticed he had inadvertently turned it off after he had made the claim. He turned it on and got only static. He tried other bands without success. He tried to communicate with both the ship and the lander with no results. The radioactivity and electrical activity on Io had increased to an elevated level.

"What was said on the last contact with the lander?" Fred asked the computer.

There was a click then the voice of the helmsman boomed, "We've noticed from your path that it'll be difficult for you to get here by nineteen hundred hours. We'll wait if possible. We've noticed increased instability on Io's surface. Further delay would put the lander in danger. Still, we've extended the departure time to nineteen thirty hours. No further delay possible." There was another click then silence.

Suddenly, Io's surface heaved and the Explorer tossed about. However, it held on and kept on course. After about two hours more, there was another much more violent quake. This one sent the Explorer tumbling onto a rocky outcropping. Fred could hear grinding and scraping sounds under the craft as it smashed heavily into some boulders.

"Position critical. Cannot get traction," were the words piped into his helmet.

Fred decided to go out and see what he could do.

It was hazardous to get out, as the Explorer was at a bad angle. Once out, Fred quickly assessed the situation. One tread was not touching the ground and the other was over a small ledge so both treads were useless. It would be impossible for the vehicle alone to resolve. Fred had to come up with a fast solution but the computer interrupted by telling him to pile rocks under the right tread. He did not hesitate in carrying out the suggestion but he could not shake the uneasy feeling he had about this additional delay. He hastily constructed a rock bridge under the tread. He was about to get up and go to the cabin when the speaker boomed again, "Not sufficient. Wedge rock into the front of the tread. Need more support. Need more traction."

It took several minutes for Fred to find a rock of enough size and wedge it under the front of the tread. When done, Fred raced into the cabin. He had been thinking of his options and had decided on another course of action. His helmet's speaker interrupted him. "Request permission to use top speed."

It was dangerous to travel at that speed even on good terrain and it was almost suicidal to do it on this terrain. He did not have much choice though. If he did not do it, there was a significant probability he would not get to the lander on time.

He jumped back into the vehicle, sat down, fastened his harness, and shouted "Permission granted."

The Explorer took off. The rapid acceleration pressed him into his seat. He used the handholds located in various places around the sides and top of the cabin. It was like being in a paint can on the shaker with all the jerking and rolling. Again and again, the Explorer passed through dangerous areas. Maybe it was luck or just their inertia keeping the vehicle going but they were making up for lost time. Fred was feeling more comfortable now as, if they kept this pace, he would get back to the landing site on time.

The voice of the computer cut into his thoughts, "Crevasse ahead, must make a detour around it. Delay will be twelve minutes."

Around the crevasse, he raced, over more bumps, into more inclines, around large rocks, swaying. This would seem like a nightmare to any man. Fred had been in similar situations three times before but he had made it on time, or the lander could delay its departure. Still, he was particularly anxious and held frantically onto the handholds for support.

The clock reached nineteen hundred and twenty-five hours. Just five more minutes, he thought. It looked as if he would make it. This sturdy little rig would bring him back just as it always had. Another tremor shook the Explorer and temporarily threw it off course. Fred knew I would soon experience a huge quake. His anxiety was changing to terror as his computer indicated his location concerning the landing site. If only there were no more delays, he thought to himself.

Still, he had not seen the lander rise into the sky. There was a chance the crew was tracking him and could see how close he was. The time was nineteen hundred hours twenty-eight minutes and forty-two seconds.

A severe quake rocked Io.

The Explorer halted its forward motion because of the danger of travelling in such conditions. It began to extend its four outriggers to stabilise the vehicle against the arrival of the full force of the quake.

Suddenly, the craft jerked severely and it flew into the air like a ball, as the ground lurched ferociously. Fred hung onto the handholds for dear life. Every other moveable object on Io's surface was also airborne. The vehicle crashed heavily onto the ground and flying rocks and boulders hit it. The tumult lasted for almost twenty minutes as the craft tossed about several more times.

Finally, the rumbling stopped and the cab became deathly quiet. Fred sat stunned by the storm that had raged around him. He passed out.

When he awoke, he turned his head slowly to the chronometer. He had been out for twenty minutes. Now, he had to assess his predicament. An aftershock, that rocked the vehicle for a few more minutes, interrupted him then quieted down.

He looked outside and noticed that the Explorer had not moved from its position. It should have resumed its journey after the storm.

He decided first to check his life needs, such as power to keep his life systems functioning. Power to the suit would be no problem as he had attached its battery to the vehicle's power source, and he could continue to do so. He knew he had about three days of food in his space suit. He tried to estimate the amount of air remaining. He noticed a loss of air from the craft's tank which must have punctured during the quake. He had already used about half of the air in his suit and spare tank, so he had about eighteen hours left there.

Now, he had to factor in one more thing – the possibility of rescue. He would have to think like a captain.

Another aftershock hit the vehicle. He was unprepared and hit his head on one of the handholds in the cabin. He had to nurse that for several minutes. He checked his gauges and was pleased his suit had not been damaged. When he had collected his wits, he began thinking about his predicament again. To help the process, he had to determine the state of the Explorer. He called out, "Computer, give me a vehicle status report."

He heard the familiar voice of the computer in his helmet. "Structural damage to personnel component. Severe damage to communications system. Power systems operative. Mobility systems operative. Hydraulic systems damaged. Computer systems damaged; have compensated using redundant parts."

"Are we able to communicate with the ship?"

"Negative."

"Is there any repair capability for the radio?"

"Negative."

"Can we repair the hydraulics?"

"Negative but systems can be operated manually."

So, what were his options? He was short of the information he needed and he could only get it by communicating with the ship or the lander. Was the ship still orbiting Io, or had it left? What about the lander? Had it survived the quake and was still waiting for him?

If the lander was damaged, the ship itself was not built to land on a surface. If the crew did try, there would be no space large enough for it to land. The risk of landing with all the aftershocks would be suicidal. Io could be unstable like this for months until it reached a new equilibrium.

Another aftershock hit but he braced himself to minimise its effect.

For several minutes, Fred just sat there but finally thought he had better get more facts. He unstrapped himself and got out of the Explorer. He peered into the sky to look for the orbiting spaceship. Five minutes went by, then another five. Had the crew changed their orbit? If not, it had left.

He looked at the Explorer. Its outriggers were still engaged. That was why it had not moved since the quake!

One by one he went to the hand crank in the small recess above each mechanism. It was tiring work and took twenty minutes to complete. He got back into the cabin and sat down. He plugged his suit back into the vehicle's power outlet and drove to the landing site.

Now, he knew why he had not seen the lander take off. Under Jupiter's glow, he could see through the viewer that the lander had toppled onto its side, splitting it along its spine. The fuel and oxygen explosion that had taken place blackened it. No one could have survived the blast. The violent quake had also strewn boulders over it, and a large crevasse beside it was spewing lava over one side. He stared glumly. There laid his lifeline; his ticket home.

He had not seen the ship, because it must have left shortly after the lander burned. There was no way the crew could have saved him; whether they thought he was dead or alive did not matter.

Fred became despondent as the full realisation engulfed him.

After his shock diminished, he took a nap there for a couple of hours. Another aftershock violently awakened him.

He sat for a few minutes to regain his senses. He programmed a destination into the computer and set the vehicle to autopilot. To break the monotony, he picked out some of his favourite music and played it through his helmet. Hours passed.

He had been in and out of sleep, eaten, and drank some more. He was no longer looking at the time. The vehicle stopped. He leaned toward the view screen to see outside. He smiled.

He got out of the vehicle and extended the outriggers. He went back in, turned off the music and turned on the recorder. "Please deliver this message to Joan Dory," and gave her identification number. A lump developed in his throat.

"Hi Joan, I don't know how to say this. I don't even know if you will get this. I have no communication with the outside world right now. I'm alone and waiting to die." He choked again and fought to continue. He had to retain his poise. This was something he had to do with some dignity but tears were welling up in his eyes. How do you say this to your wife? How do you say this to someone you love; to someone you realise you don't know, as your marriage is so new, and to someone with whom you share a child who will now never see you?

"I guess you were right. I'm sorry for what I said about your getting pregnant. I've accepted it, especially when I've seen him grow up from afar. He's going to be quite some fellow. Maybe it was some intuition that made you do it. I wanted to be a father and my parents wanted to have grandchildren, so you fulfilled those dreams but I never thought anything like this would happen to me. I'm not going to get out of this and get back to you . . . sorry." He sniffled.

Through his hoarse voice, he continued, "Take care of Marshal. I'm sorry he won't have a father now."

He had to stop and regain his composure.

He continued. "Ever since you told me you were pregnant, I longed to get back to you and him and help you raise him. All the money I have can't give me the pleasure I would have had living with you and our little boy. Almost the whole trip, I was thinking of all the things I would do when I got back. I could have spent all my time with the two of you. Now, I'll never see you or him again . . . I have no idea when, or if, anyone will come here to pick up this message and get it to you but if they do, know that I love you very much and I want you to be happy despite what happened.

"In my will, I have left half my wealth to you . . . although I know it's no consolation but it should make you comfortable until you can restart your life. I know our parents will be there to support you."

He stopped again for a few minutes as he broke down. He needed to close this conversation but struggled. Finally, he collected the energy to say, "Goodbye Joan, give a warm hug and kiss to Marshal for me. Tell him I love him, no matter how old he will be when this gets to you. And for you, whatever you make of your life, I wish you the very best. I love you so much and I hope you can find it in your heart to find someone who can give you as much, or more, love than I had for you for the brief time we've known each other. All I want is for you to be happy . . . End message."

Now for the next task. Fred waited until his tears had stopped before he continued, "Please deliver this message to Marshal and Elizabeth Dory," and gave their numbers. He paused. "Hi Mom, hi Dad; I don't know when, or if, this message will get to you but I thought I would leave you with a few words from way out here in the Jupiter system. SEM will execute my will and I have left half of all I have to you. Please use the money to live comfortably and do all the travelling you would have liked to have done and would not have had the resources to do.

"I know you had other plans for me and had explained to me the hazards of life in space but this was my chosen career. I guess I had to go on one more trip; one more adventure, before I settled down. I guess you'll at least have the satisfaction of fulfilling your dream of my marrying and having a grandchild for you . . . This was going to be my last trip, though . . . All I could think of throughout my journey was getting back home to you, Joan, and little Marshal. I could see the joy you had with him when we communicated and I saw you all at Christmas . . . I guess I won't be able to see any of you, now.

"Having a son has also made me realise what it's like to be a father and how it must feel to lose a child. No parent can conceive of having someone you brought up as a baby die before you do. I'm sorry I put you through this.

"I love you both very much. Thank you for everything you have done for me, for all the diapers you must have changed . . ." Fred chuckled, ". . . for your advice and counsel through the years, and mostly for your love . . . Hugs and kisses, Fred. End message."

He sat for a few minutes trying to compose himself. This task was more difficult than he thought it would be, and he was struggling to keep his composure.

"Please deliver this message to the senior personnel officer of the System Exploration and Mining Inc." Fred paused. "Sandra Bell, or whoever will be in the position when this message gets there; please accept my apologies for what happened on Io. The decisions leading to my demise were totally mine and I absolve the crew of all blame. They did all in their power to avoid the incident or come to my aid. Conditions on Io were too dangerous to enable any rescue. Please copy my sentiments to the crew. Please execute my will and life insurance, if you have not done it already. Fred Dory. End message."

He leaned back satisfied, and turned on the music again. Somehow the messages he had prepared to his family seemed to calm him as he hoped they would someday get back to his loved ones. Another aftershock shook him. He ate a little more mush, drank a little water, and enjoyed the music.

When the needle on the air tank dropped into the red zone, a light began to blink in a corner of his faceplate. He found it difficult to concentrate on the music. He began to consider ending his life now by using the cyanide capsule he could take within the suit but that did not sit well with him.

When the air ran out, his symptoms came quickly. He was finding it difficult to breathe now. The carbon dioxide was building up in the suit and the oxygen was depleting. He knew the end was near.

Amidst the majestic music, his thoughts were of his life and parents; his childhood games of war and good days with his friends, when he pretended to be in the space force, then his joining space cadets, and his entering university. He smiled as he thought of his marriage and frowned at his decision to return to SEM to go to Jupiter. He longed to hold the son he would never meet and never know. He remembered his work with SEM and felt pride in it but was embarrassed by this error. It took only one mistake to create a situation like this. The only consolation he had was, at least, that he would leave a fortune to his wife and parents in his will. He came out of his daydream with a terrible headache. The music continued to provide some distraction and he focused harder on it.

He developed an overpowering urge to rip off the faceplate to get fresh air. He began to panic. It took tremendous willpower to resist this urge and keep his sanity. He did not want to die. His body was fighting for its life. He was breathing furiously, his heart was racing, and he felt flushed. He was losing his focus and was unsure where he was. He blacked out. His heart continued to race futilely for several seconds more but Fred was no longer there.

* * *

Bill Johnson, the engineer, hooked up a power cable to the Explorer. He began looking through the vehicle's computer files. "So, he was late because of a large pile of platinum and gold, huh?"

"Looks that way. That's what the ship's cook reported at the time," answered Jed Hornsby, the helmsman. "The ship's captain who left him here couldn't save him. Fred had become a friend of his over the years and it must have been hard to leave without him. Fred was so close; apparently, he was not far from the lander when all hell broke loose."

"Yeah, too bad for old Fred. I'll copy the computer records. There are some messages here . . . Okay, done."

"Not much solace now. Let's report in."

"He's pretty well preserved, isn't he, just a little shrivelled up?"

"Yeah, space suits do that."

"Should we go now?"

"Yeah."

The two of them pulled Fred from the Explorer and loaded him, and the nugget of gold, into the back of their vehicle.

"All right, let's get off this ore bed and back to our lander," Jed suggested.

"I guess some people have their reasons for returning to places of their greatest happiness. He could have just stayed at the site of the original landing."

"Yeah, the trip back to the ore bed must have been treacherous but I guess it didn't matter if he died here or at the landing site."

Bill went over to the piles of gold and platinum, reached down, picked up two large chunks of the metal and said, "We may as well collect a souvenir for each of us while we're here."

They took one more look at the tonnes of gleaming gold, platinum, and other metals around them then got into their vehicle. "We're on our way," Bill continued.

"I guess it's worth the trip to bury him at home with his family and friends rather than just leave him here by himself in the middle of nowhere."

They looked at their souvenirs.

"How silly, going after a lot of worthless ore," Bill said with a sigh.

"Yeah, but remember this happened thirty-six years ago. This was worth something then."

"I suppose so. Now we'll keep our nuggets only as paperweights."

"If only he'd known that, about a year after their ship left Jupiter, the platinum, gold, and other precious metals market collapsed. A new large mine in South America and the arrival of the last ship of ore from the asteroids destabilised the market. Precious metals lost twenty per cent in the first six months, then paused for a couple of months until the hoarders and speculators finally panicked and sent it into free fall. The new mine closed and the ore shipment from the asteroids and the almost full ship of ore from Jupiter is still orbiting Earth. I've heard one millionaire used gold instead of copper for the water pipes in his new house."

"Yeah, what a shame he lost his life for nothing."

"Do you want to know what happened on the expedition?"

"You know more?"

"Yes, when I found out we were going to pick up this guy, I did some digging and read up on the story.

"Because the ship had left Jupiter later than planned, the crew had to plot a much longer flight plan. They could have decreased their mass by dumping the ore and keeping the old plan but none of them wanted to do that.

"As they were leaving orbit, they struck a large rock outside of Jupiter's orbital plane that tore a huge hole in the front end of the ship, destroyed the ship's communications dish, and threw them off their trajectory. Two people died in the accident as they happened to be in that part of the ship when it occurred. They had no more contact with Earth and lost some fuel and supplies. They had to spend some time and fuel to correct their course.

"When mission control on earth lost contact with the ship, they thought everyone had died but they kept an eye on the ship's progress and, in time, determined it had made several corrective manoeuvres along its journey. When it got closer to Earth, Moon Base realised the ship was not slowing enough, so they sent out several spaceships to rendezvous with the ship to connect to it and use their rockets to slow it down.

"When they finally got inside the ship, only three people were still alive, the two remaining scientists and one crew member, the cook but they were in pretty bad shape. Even with only four people left after the crash with the rock, they ran out of food because of the added length of their journey.

"From what I read, after the market crash, people who had invested in the mining industry went from riches to rags overnight. I read that Fred lost every dollar he had and his estate evaporated after taxes and expenses. When SEM went bankrupt, the trustee had no money to cover Fred's, or any other employees', life insurance. You know regular life insurance companies do not cover space travellers or workers.

His parents had wanted his body brought home and had paid to do so. Because of the high cost of doing that, he ended up leaving his parents deeply in debt. Even with the money they had spent, they could not have his body immediately collected but only when there was a spaceship conveniently near Jupiter. They died before they could pick him up, so they ended up never seeing their son again and died in poverty and heartbreak.

"Fred's wife also lost her money but she went back to live with her parents for a few years then remarried.

"The ship's survivors had a huge surprise being out of contact with Earth and landing at the space station loaded with worthless ore. Fortunately, some good people scraped up the funds to pay their fares back to Earth. The two remaining scientists were able to recoup their dignity with the research data, and lab specimens, they had brought back with them from Jupiter and its satellites."

"Well, it's a bit of a sad story. I hope we get off Io soon before we meet the same fate as Fred. This place looks a little like Hell would look like to me. Three people have already died here."

* * *

There was a knock at the door. The middle-aged man got up from his easy chair and opened it.

"Mom, how are you? What brings you here? You didn't call. I haven't seen you for a couple of weeks."

"Hi, Marshal, I've been busy for the last week or so."

"Oh, anything I should know?"

"For a few days, I've been thinking about what I should do."

"About what?" He was listening carefully. "Why don't you come in and sit down and we can talk about it? Where's Dad?"

"I thought I'd come alone."

He closed the door and the two of them sat in the family room. Marshal's wife, Meg, entered the room.

"Hi, Joan, nice to see you. The kids are all asleep in bed, so Marshal will have some quiet. I caught a bit of the end of your conversation. Do you want to talk in private?"

"No, I don't think so. Both of you should hear what I have to say."

Joan continued. "It's about your dad . . . your real dad. He's been brought back from Io."

"Oh, they made it. They wouldn't say if they would do it for sure."

"Yes, they've kept him for a few weeks until everyone can have time to gather whomever we need for the rites and burial."

"It's nice you kept a copy of the video communications you had with him on his journey. At least I had a chance to see him and know a little about him. I treasure them," Marshal said sadly.

"What we never knew was what happened to him. The last thing I heard from him was he was going down to the surface of Io to check out some promising precious metal mines. He was very excited about it. Apparently, on his way back, the ship lost contact with him, there was a severe quake that destroyed the lander, and its two crew members in one gigantic blast from the ignition of the ship's fuel. The crew of the spaceship reported back they weren't sure what happened to your father but they suspected he died in the quake. The little ground vehicle wasn't severely damaged, so they were sure the body was intact. That's why the parents wanted to bring back his corpse. As you know, soon after that, Earth lost contact with the ship."

"So, Dad's home." He sighed. "When's the funeral?"

"In a little more than a week but that's not why I'm here. He left something behind I never expected. I've been thinking a lot about whether I should tell you."

"He left something? Why wouldn't you want me to hear about it?"

"Because he didn't die during the quake, Son. He wasn't killed instantly."

"Oh . . . Marshal's face saddened. "He lived a couple of days or so after the quake?"

"Something like that."

"It must have been horrible then. What could he leave behind?"

"A message. You may not want to hear it."

"Oh," Marshal said nothing for several minutes. Did he want to hear the words of a dying man, especially if they were from his father?

"You don't need to do it. All he wanted me to tell you was he loved you and he's sorry he couldn't be a father for you."

"Maybe that's all I should know then." He finally relented and decided to hear what his father had to say. He took the small cube from his mother and popped it into his ear.

His mother watched his eyes fill with tears as he listened to the message.

"How did he die?" he said with a sob.

"He ran out of air."

"What a way to die."

"In the end, he not only didn't bring home a treasure, he lost whatever treasure he had at home.

"Wealth is nothing, son. Life and love were his greatest treasures and he left his greatest legacy here on Earth . . . you."

Marshal's head drooped as she continued. "You can hold on to his last words to you, and the nugget I have in this bag." She pulled out the nugget his father had collected for a souvenir, "and keep the other messages you have." She paused. "Do you want me to stay awhile?"

"No, Mom . . . It's okay. Thanks for bringing this to me."

"Finally, here's the hug he wanted me to give to you."

The two of them cried silently while they held tightly to each other.

FOUNDER

If my memory serves me right, I thought of this story around 1995. Here, a mother takes her son to the planetary museum to teach him about the evolution of their planet. I developed the details as I went along. The end was a surprise, even to me.

Margo woke up excitedly. Today, his mother was taking him to the World Museum. His father was attending a conference in Capital City and brought his family along. He and his wife, Marla, had been to the city several times but this would be the first time for their son.

Margo was ten years old but his profound knowledge of world history belied his age. While most youngsters had their minds filled with fairy tales, his mother had told him about the real tales of their planet's civilisation; how life had evolved and how humankind had emerged on the scene with their innate proclivity for war and destruction.

She filled him in on how early city-states had developed, followed by the amalgamation over time of city-states of common origin into countries, ultimately leading to the creation of a world government. He was fascinated by the wonderful stories of the exploits of those heroes and wars, malfeasance, and evil. So, when his mother told him about their trip and the museums that he would be able to see, he was ecstatic, as this was also the site of the Obelisk, the holiest of all the shrines to their past.

Margo had helped plan the trip with his mother and had helped her pack. Since the journey was taking place during the school year, he had had to get a release from school for those days but there had been no problem getting it as he was a straight 'A' student. He would also present a report to the class about his trip. He had enjoyed the aeroplane ride and had been excited about staying in a hotel. He had not had a good night's sleep, though, as he had been too thrilled about the trip to the museum.

On the first day, while his father was at the conference, Margo and his mother had a delicious breakfast and had a nice trip on the tour bus to the World Museum. It fascinated the young man. It laid out the history of their planet from the evolution of the first life forms to intelligent life, focusing on the history of their civilisation. The museum was so large he also spent the next two days there examining the displays, dioramas, and holographs. It was a tremendous learning experience for him. Some of it he had learned from his mother or at school but there was much new material to excite and hold his interest.

On the last day, he was particularly keyed up. This was the day he was going to the Obelisk. His mother's stories had not included this remarkable story, as she had reserved this for when he was older and more mature. She had only told him there was an Obelisk and earlier peoples had worshipped it because they did not understand what it was, so he knew it existed and was very important.

When they got off the tour bus, he and his mother stood for several minutes in front of the building housing the Obelisk. They were fascinated by its facade. The stone front with its highly ornate carvings was spectacular. There were no other buildings on the planet that could match the intricacy and beauty of this building. He had seen a picture of it but no photograph or even a three-dimensional image could compare to seeing it in real life. At their approach, the large heavy door of the building opened ponderously. The interior was essentially one huge room, with the Obelisk in the centre of it. The room was considerably simpler in design than the outside to match more closely with the stark simplicity of the Obelisk. Around the walls were many descriptive plaques.

His mother took him on a plaque-by-plaque tale of the beginnings of their planet. She had passed through this building many times in her life, both during school and afterwards. She paraphrased the writings on the plaques as they passed in front of them while he read along.

"Shortly after our planet formed billions of years ago, it had an atmosphere consisting principally of carbon dioxide, nitrogen and water. As our planet was relatively close to our young sun, it was hot and slowly lost its water over the billions of years as it broke down into hydrogen and oxygen. The hydrogen, because it was so light, left our planet. The free oxygen is combined with carbon, sulphur, or iron. Because carbon dioxide holds in the heat, our planet became very hot, so hot that no life could exist. That process continued for four and a half billion years. What remained was an essentially waterless, lifeless, and rocky planet with temperatures of several hundred degrees Celsius covered by thick clouds of sulphur oxides."

She paused as they walked to the next section of the displays.

"Then, here's where it gets interesting for you. Some people came to visit our planet and saw hope in it. Not much is known of these people anymore as our planet has evolved for over two billion years since then, and there's no longer much trace of them. The little we know of them comes from the Obelisk and many cases from theories, and guesses but what we have so far, is their technology must have been beyond what we have today.

"There is evidence on our planet of a huge cataclysm that occurred around that time, a catastrophe so great it almost destroyed the planet. A huge asteroid, moon, comet, or planetoid struck at such a velocity and angle as to cause a drastic change in the spin of our planet, speeding it up. We believe the purpose of this faster speed of rotation was to give our planet a magnetic field. In other words, our scientists have guessed the object was deliberately crashed into our planet."

Margo interrupted his mother. "Why do that if it almost destroyed our planet? They could have gone too far and destroyed it."

"Yes, that's right. That could have happened but the best we can postulate is our new magnetic field gave us a level of protection from cosmic rays by deflecting them into space. Some evidence shows that objects, or maybe several objects, also gave our planet enough water to dilute the acid in the atmosphere and start trapping some of the carbon dioxide in the air.

"Another thing we have some evidence for is that they put an object into orbit around our star that shaded our planet from its heat to reduce the temperature. It also served as an ion collector that focused a beam of hydrogen ions onto our planet to replace the hydrogen it was losing to ionisation from our planet's upper atmosphere. We once sent a spacecraft to an object now orbiting the sun which looks very much like that instrument. It stopped functioning over a billion or more years ago but, by then, it had served its purpose.

"Now this is where things become quite murky and our scientists are making educated guesses. Our founders used bacteria and algae of some sort which may have existed on their planet, or were perhaps bioengineered organisms, and dispersed tonnes of these organisms into our atmosphere to photosynthesise the carbon dioxide into carbohydrates and oxygen and perhaps also to reduce the sulphur dioxide and trioxide in our atmosphere into sulphur. The oxygen would have reacted with the hydrogen ions, creating more water, and providing the basis for the beginning of life. Reducing the amount of carbon dioxide and sulphuric acid in the atmosphere would also have reduced its acidity over time. The organisms would likely have found a more-or-less habitable band in our atmosphere in which to live and begin to perform their function. As the planet became more habitable, the microbes would have continued to accelerate the work of improving the planet.

"Two and a half billion years of planetary evolution generated enough free oxygen in the atmosphere for an ozone layer to develop. This, plus our new magnetic field, would have protected our planet from cosmic rays and ultraviolet light, as well as provided us with the living plants and animals we have with us now. Another factor is, over time, our star cooled, which would also have helped in giving us a more moderate temperature and weather."

The dioramas ended, now. They walked to the Obelisk in the centre of the building and stood before it. It was a silver-coloured reflective tower standing about eight meters high. Margo's mother read the last small plaque while adding more details.

"Was this a monument to vanity? We are not sure but it did perform one additional function. When the atmospheric temperature dropped to a liveable level for an extended time, a compartment in the Obelisk opened and released something from inside of it. We think it was plant seeds to accelerate the evolutionary process.

"The Obelisk was a very special vessel. Someone made it of a very durable material; a type of plastic impervious to our former hot and corrosive atmosphere. Scientists think it is silver in colour to reflect radiant heat to try to keep the insides cooler, and may have had a simple long-lasting cooling mechanism to protect its contents from the searing heat of our atmosphere at the time, to prevent the seeds inside from being baked.

"Look over there and you'll see the opening in the Obelisk that must have contained the seeds." She pointed to the area on the Obelisk where a dark opening was visible. They walked there.

"When our early people first found the Obelisk, they worshipped it like a temple to God. They had had no history that any people on this planet had made it and it contained a strange unknown material. In time, they built a city around it, then this magnificent building. It stands where it always stood and where it always will. The Founders placed it on high ground which they knew would be above the oceans which would form as the planet evolved.

Margo raised his hand with another puzzling question. "Why would those people have done all this for us?"

"That's a big question for us. Our scientists have travelled in space to search for their planet but after over two billion years there is very little evidence they even existed. We have seen some traces of them but not enough to get a true idea of who they were and what they were like, so to determine their motive would be extremely hypothetical. Did they do it solely for their purposes, for example, to take it over as another place for them to live themselves? They appear to have disappeared. Did they perhaps become extinct before our planet became habitable for them?

"Did they do it for altruistic reasons, just to create a new liveable planet for life to evolve to create new beings in the universe?

"Did they do it as a commercial venture to exploit the planet and its animals and people? We will never know unless they moved away and will return to visit us to collect some expected reward. Who knows? There are many ideas but no one knows the correct reason.

"So, Margo, these people are our greatest heroes. They gave us our big start. Without them, our planet would still be a steamy, desolate place."

"So, we don't know anything about the Founders, and what they were like?" Margo reiterated.

"We do know some things we learned from the Obelisk, from the markings on it. That is why many people think it was also a monument to the act they performed. It may mean they were a proud people. It is the greatest remaining artefact indicating these people even existed. The orbiting shading device has no meaningful markings on it. Other than some footprints in the dust and artefacts on some of the planets and moons of our solar system, this is all we have left of them.

"Come over here and look at these markings." She pointed to another spot on the Obelisk on the opposite side to where the dark depression was.

He squinted to try to read them but they did not make any sense to him. "What does it say, mother?"

"Nobody knows but the drawings on it tell us a lot. You can see the main part of the picture is of a solar system. If you compare it to a schematic of our solar system, they match closely enough to tell us they are the same. You can see a mark beside the third planet, so we surmise they are telling us that is where they came from, in other words, they must have come from our solar system, too. There are names besides the planets. They named their planet 'Earth' and ours 'Venus'. Under the picture are the symbols 'Project funded under the auspices of the Bill Gates Foundation' but we don't know what it means. Those must be characters that formed their language."

Margo interrupted, "If I remember what I learned in school, the third planet is barren. It was destroyed long ago by overheating by carbon dioxide."

"But you also remember we are in the process of recovering it, although we did not have as much difficulty as they did with us. It should only be a few thousand years before we will have it liveable again. It already has an ozone layer, a gravitational field, and water. The planet has been working hard to correct the situation of the planet's runaway greenhouse gases, garbage pollution, etc. We must help it along. We won't be able to reset the same carbon dioxide level it originally had, however, as a higher level is necessary due to the sun's reduction in heat output since that time."

Margo stood pensively for a few minutes then added, "It seems odd to me they could achieve the monumental task of remaking our planet when they could not even save their own."

"You are wise beyond your years, my son. That is our biggest question."

THE BET

I am not sure when I thought of this story. It was originally a simple story about an experiment by some scientists called "The Jupiter Effect" but as I began to write it, my fingers got a little out of control and I ended up with a love story added to it. Despite this, or because of it, I hope you like it.

Troy had finally made it. After six years of challenging work, he had gained tenure. Besides that, he had become one of the university's most popular chemistry teachers with students and faculty. Moreover, he was single, quite handsome, and a favourite with the eligible female staff. Because of his dedication to his work, he was not interested in their advances. He tended to ignore them and treated them like one of the boys.

However, one young woman, a physicist, had him in her sights and had at least gotten to the point of meeting for a few lunches, visits to local restaurants, and even to her apartment for a home-cooked supper.

One day, they were in the staff lounge conversing with a mathematician and a geologist. At one point, they drifted into a discussion of a rather interesting question, one that had stymied scientists for many years.

The physicist and geologist believed the event was quite probable, while the mathematician and Troy were quite adamant it was virtually impossible. At one point, the argument got quite heated, so the big question became, could they come up with some proof one way or another? That ignited another discussion over the possibility of even coming up with a probability factor for such an occurrence. The conversation went into the evening, ending up as a draw.

After a brief pause of a few minutes in the conversation, the physicist decided to get the group really into the issue, using a wager. "I think we have a lot of talent in the room. I think we can develop a methodology to determine, with a reasonable probability, an answer to the question. To increase our chances of resolving the issue, we can solicit the aid of other scientists. I'm certain that if we are successful, this should increase our esteem in the science community and we may be able to issue one or more publications. To make it even more interesting, I propose we make a bet. I also propose it be a mystery bet but it must be substantial.

"The mystery part is we put our wager onto a slip of paper, fold it, put it into an envelope, and place it into a box we can seal and give to a third party for safekeeping. For the substantial part, we could write down that the loser must have to pay $100,000 or has to work on a research project for the winner for three months, or six months, or it could require the loser to sit on a tall pole in the middle of the campus for a week or two or something like that."

"Oh, yes, I'm sure if someone asked you to pole-sit in public you'd do it," Troy said sceptically.

"If we solved this problem, I'd be in such a celebratory mood, I think I would." She went on, "What I'm trying to get across to you is we have to keep the bet."

"But we don't know what it's going to be," interjected the mathematician.

"That's the mystery. The bets would also be individual. For example, I would have to set my bet with the two losers. If I wrote $100,000 to one loser, that person would have to pay me $100,000, and if I wrote the other loser would work with me on a project for four hours a day for six months, that person would do that. Just for fun, at the end, we could announce what the bets would have been for the losers."

The three men were muttering to each other. This was the strangest wager they had ever heard of. The geologist was the first to respond. "I think this is a little childish. Why can't we have no bets at all and just give the project a good try, or agree upfront on what the prizes will be? Why use this mystery approach?"

Troy was quiet for a while then said, "Yes, it's strange. I've never heard of a wager as odd as this but it may be fun."

"But all the bets will almost certainly be different. Somebody may put in a small bet, another person put down a substantial bet," responded the mathematician.

The men started to argue among themselves.

"Why don't we vote?" interrupted the physicist to get the discourse back to the point.

There was grumbling from the others.

"Okay, who is in favour of my wagering system?" the physicist asked.

She and Troy raised their hands.

"Who is against?" she demanded.

The geologist's hand went up.

"Why didn't you put up your hand?" she asked the mathematician, puzzled.

"If I put my hand up there'll be a tie. What happens if there's a tie?"

"I guess we'd have to figure out what else to do, do normal betting, draw straws, drop it entirely, or whatever."

"We can end up discussing it all night. I don't care one way or the other so I'll break the tie."

"Okay, because it's getting late, let's make the wager another time. You can have time to think about it."

Everyone agreed to that suggestion. The next discussion was the size of the team they would need. They finally decided that they needed four extra members: a statistician, a computer programmer, a cellular biologist, and an astronomer. Each of them would solicit a person in these faculties and encourage him or her to join the team; however, they would not participate in the wager. The first four professors they approached turned out to be very interested in coming on board.

The next evening, the eight professors met in the lounge to make a rough plan. Troy worked through the next morning to record the plan and make some refinements to it. The next evening, the group met to hone the plan further then, using brainstorming techniques, they identified all the factors they thought may influence the subject area. They included some factors that they were not sure would have an effect but they should include, just in case. They then parcelled out the tasks to people who would likely be able to get the data associated with the factors. For example, the geologist would gather data associated with the Earth, such as its gravity, composition, etc. The computer programmer and statistician had no task at that point.

After the four non-betting scientists left, the other four placed their bets into a small box and the physicist sealed it with wax.

One week later, they met with all the data collected and this time they presented, analysed, and discussed how to fit everything together. In some cases, they felt some additional data was required but for the most part, the information looked sufficient. They agreed to break up into smaller groups to refine the data and the interactions with the other factors. The mathematician and the statistician were involved in all the groups to help with that process.

Meanwhile, the computer programmer was arranging with his faculty, and many volunteers, to assemble a bank of linked computers to help with some of the calculations. He also obtained permission to use the university's computer system but he could use it only during the evenings and weekends, as he was expecting a huge computational demand because of the calculations necessary to consider all the combinations and permutations necessary to complete the task.

The next week, they met again and discussed what they had at that point. They thought that a static portrayal of the data may not present an accurate view of reality, so they gathered more data to account for changes over time. The geologist groaned over the additional data he had to gather. The statistician and mathematician were complaining over how much more complicated the algorithms were going to be and the added time it would take to set up the calculations. They agreed that simulations would be the best way of dealing with the probability analysis.

For months, the team worked and the program evolved as the factors changed. In the end, the mathematician and statistician set up the analysis and the computer programmer wrote the routines needed to run the simulations.

It was testing day, 18 months after the four professors first discussed the proposal.

"Well, team," stated the physicist, "it's been an amazing start to the project. Everyone has worked very hard. It's been a challenge and there were moments when I thought everyone was going to give up but here, we are, at a critical point in our project. I think we all deserve a pat on the back. We're ready to run the program and see if it works. We won't know how long it'll take to get our first set of results."

Troy took over talking. "I've put everyone's name into this old hat and I'll pick out one name from it for the person who's going to push the enter key to start the simulation." He stuck his hand into the hat and pulled out a slip of paper. "Hey, look who won – the big man who did the programming. I think it's fitting."

The computer programmer reached over and pressed the key. At first, everyone watched in anticipation until one of them reminded everyone else the routine could take days. The programmer then told everyone he would keep an eye on the computer and notify them when it was complete.

Three days later, the team got a call, and one hour later everyone assembled to hear the news. They did not get the results they expected.

"It can't be," said the cellular biologist.

"Well, we'll have to look at our assumptions and see if there are any flaws," Troy retorted. "Did we put in something we shouldn't have, or missed something?"

"But the work in doing that is intense. We may be at it for a week, or even more," responded the mathematician.

"We can take it in chunks with different people taking different pieces," advised the statistician.

The physicist cut in, "I'm ready to bet our historical data is the most likely area of error."

"Oh, no, not more betting!" the mathematician said with a sigh.

"It was only a figure of speech," the physicist responded hastily. "We're getting a little hypersensitive. I think maybe we should break off now and review all our data and see where we need to make changes. We've got to make sure we have everything in there, every tiny piece of history. I know that's a lot but we may miss the mark with one tiny detail we forgot. We're not sure what the critical components are."

Everyone began to leave. Some of the team started to work on their area of the project right after the meeting, digging up tiny details they may have missed in the first round. Others decided to leave the work for another day. In the end, they all returned to the lounge one week later with the results. The geologist added eighty- three new parameters to the equation, the astronomer thirty -four and the biologist three.

Now, it was up to the statistician, mathematician, and programmer to analyse the information and work them into the equations then the computer programs. They tried another run without success. After six months of repeated testing, the whole team became disheartened. They had tried eleven times to get their scenario to work. The first three or four tests served to debug the program. If the scenario did not work then they would not be able to execute the second series of tests.

The team met to review carefully their assumptions and dates of certain events.

"We've been stymied for six months of testing now and I know you're getting frustrated," Troy led with a sigh. "I still think we can find the answer. We shouldn't give up. The problem may be in our data, or the simulation program. We may be too close to the project now to look for weaknesses. With your permission, I would like to approach other people to take a complete look at what we've done and get their input."

"I'm willing to do anything to move the project forward. I knew it wasn't going to be an easy task," the mathematician cut in.

"Who do you think we can approach?" responded the geologist. "As far as I know, I've covered everything possible from my end. Maybe a palaeontologist would be a suitable candidate, particularly at the assumptions I've made. As a geologist, I know a lot about palaeontology but that is not my specialty. There are myriads of permutations we're looking at, and there may be many more than we've assumed. I can get a hold of someone who may be the person to do the job."

"My work in statistics and probability I believe is sound but there may be something I left out. It's crucial to get everything very precise. I know someone who may be good to go over what I have done so far," added the statistician.

The physicist questioned eagerly, "Does anyone else have any other suggestions?"

There was silence.

Troy ended the meeting with, "At least this is a good start. I think those areas are good to look at first. Meanwhile, I want everyone to look at what they've done, plus look at what others have done as well, so we can be sure we've done everything possible to obtain some results on the next test."

Two weeks later, the team met again. The statistician presented the report from his colleague and indicated they had come up with several improvements to the scenario's calculations which he had already passed on to the computer programmer. The geologist had a lengthy list of changes due to the results of recent studies and many newly added items. He had verified the data and even added some items himself.

The programmer had found a few program glitches that, from his point of view, would not have affected the results but if improved, would speed up processing the data. He had also found more volunteers to add their computers into his network to help the processing speed, although, with each new iteration of the program it was having to do increased calculations as the processing got more complex.

It took a week to make all the changes. The next week, they ran the program. When they got together to examine the results, they were excited. They did not get the results they wanted but they had received a very promising start. They finished step one but they decided not to celebrate.

The geologist, astronomer, and physicist held a meeting with the palaeontologist the next day.

The geologist spoke to the palaeontologist first. "So, what do you think of the results?"

"Wow, it's a good start. I thought I had put everything into the pot. I went over my data again but can't think of anything else. We've got such a mass of conditions right now. We've also included changes over time. It's amazing what we've done. We've now probably got the largest collection of data on this subject ever amassed in one place. Even that's worth a paper in some journal."

"I wonder where our errors are and what we've missed?" the physicist added.

"Have we accounted for all the asteroids and comets?" mused the astronomer.

"Would that make much of a difference? We've put in most of the major ones," responded the palaeontologist.

"And they all must be at the correct period," added the astronomer, "and we have to make sure the masses are correct."

"Maybe we should add the mass that impacted the moon. It would change its mass through time also," continued the palaeontologist.

"Would that make any difference?" the physicist mumbled.

133

"Who knows?" questioned the palaeontologist with a sigh. "We're brain-storming here. Let's keep the juices flowing."

"I agree," said the physicist, "We'll discover later what details are relevant, or not. Right now, let's add whatever we can to the equations. I'd love to get it to work. We've come so close."

"There are so many unknowns. We may miss some of the smaller bodies that have impacted on the Earth or Moon," stated the astronomer.

"We can only deal with what we know," added the physicist.

"I can also add the gravitational effects of Mars and Venus but that will take some time to gather," continued the astronomer.

"That's a good idea," the physicist supported.

"I can dig up whatever else I can and get back to you," closed the palaeontologist.

"And, so will we," responded the geologist and astronomer. They put on their coats and marched into the wintery evening.

Three weeks later, they collected all the data and added it to the rest of the information. They ran the test again but still without the results they were expecting; however, they could see improvements in them.

The whole group sat frustratedly and quietly in their chairs in the staff lounge.

The physicist opened the meeting. "Everyone looks so gloomy. I know it still hasn't worked the way we expected but we should be looking at what we've achieved. We've at least proved the first part of our objective. It'll be tougher to get to the second stage. The third stage will likely be longer."

There was silence for several minutes.

Troy tried to pick up their resolve, "Come on, what would Thomas Edison have thought of us? He never gave up. Let's just start thinking of ideas. What more can you think of to add to all the data we have now? We've looked at everything associated with the sun, and the moon, and even added in Mars and Venus just in case; after all, they're Earth's nearest neighbours. We've looked at everything we know about the Earth, from its mass and tilt to its composition and structure."

There was more silence.

"Maybe our system is too static," the astronomer broke the silence.

"We've accounted for the changes over time," Troy ventured.

"Yes, but other things are happening in the solar system. How we've designed our scenarios right now is we have the Earth going around the sun with rocks hitting it. Sure, we have tectonic plates moving and banging into each other but we haven't put the rest of the solar system into the equation."

"Everything else is so far away they would have no effect on our results, except for the sun of course, and we've taken the sun well into account in the scenarios," the physicist added.

"What about Jupiter?" the astronomer countered.

"What about it? The distance from it to the Earth is so great, even though it's the largest planet, it would not have any effect on the Earth," replied the physicist.

"I agree but it influences other things that affect the process and there are other effects too. For example, if it was much larger, it would have ignited and become a star, making our solar system a double star system, and that would have had a huge effect. If it was much smaller, another thing would have occurred. The solar system would have had

135

another planet instead of the asteroid belt. As it is, Jupiter prevented the other planet from forming or caused one to break up. It can still perturb the belt enough to have asteroids ejected from it. It may be that many of the asteroids that hit the moon and our planet most recently were from the belt. Asteroids or other phenomena have made substantial changes to Earth and the other planets."

"Oh?"

"If everyone agrees, can we make those changes to the simulation so it could take all that into account?"

Everyone nodded their heads. There was nothing to lose.

"Does anyone else have any other suggestions?"

There was silence.

They all agreed to download all the added data, make the changes to the program the astronomer had offered, and run the test.

They all left to get a good night's sleep, except for the astronomer, and Troy, who had decided to stay back and work on the calculations.

It took them two weeks to finish the work. Then, the programmer spent the next week getting the information into the program.

Everyone gathered for its launch. They had put so much into it. This had to be it. The programmer had rigged up a large button so it would act as a return key on the keyboard to allow everyone to push it at the same time and launch the program.

Four days later, the programmer called everyone together to announce the results. There was apprehension in the room as the programmer arrived late with a USB stick in his hand.

He plopped it on the table in the middle of the room. The physicist and the mathematician slid the stick into its spot in the computer and huddled over the monitor. Smiles were appearing on everyone's faces.

When they finished, the physicist said, "We've done it. The timing is not perfect but we've done it. This is amazing. The astronomer was correct, I guess. Jupiter's effect pulled everything together."

Troy left the room and about ten minutes later walked in with two bottles of champagne. The group celebrated.

When the celebrating diminished, Troy called for quiet. "As you know, the project is not complete. This point was crucial to completing the project but now phase three begins and this will be the longest continuous run. It may take many weeks to finish and, thanks to lots of volunteers for their computers, we can keep it as short as possible. I suggest that everyone try to put the project out of our minds for now and get back to the projects we're supposed to be working on. We'll be notified, as usual, when the routines are done and we know the answer."

The programmer announced he would go right over to the laboratory and start the run for the final analysis.

They were all patting each other on the back as they filed out of the room.

Finally, the big day arrived and the programmer sent out a message to the eight partners that the results were in.

The group met again but this time in a small conference room to give them more privacy.

The programmer opened the meeting. "Hi, everyone, I'm sure you are anxious to find out the results, so I'll get to them quickly. I carefully examined them. The summary is on the first five pages of the report, the rest are just the minute details of the calculations. The bottom line is, the event is almost impossible."

"I've lost the bet," the physicist said.

Troy jumped up, "Hurray!" He scrambled to the computer monitor and scanned through the first five pages. Each of the others followed suit.

When everyone had settled down, the physicist placed four envelopes on the table.

The mathematician paused and questioned, "Are these results irrefutable?"

Troy responded, "Not really but they're going to be hard to challenge. You can prove something exists but you cannot prove something does not, so that applies here. Maybe there are other factors that, when put into the scenarios, will get opposite results but until then, this is the model, and you better believe that, once we publish the results, there will be many scientists trying to challenge us. That's science. I hope our results will stand at least for a year or so. For now, let's just be happy and celebrate what we have achieved and look at our bets. That was the arrangement."

The mathematician added, "I think we covered so much, I can't see how anyone will ever come up with another solution. There are just so many factors involved. What we have proved is, that even accounting for the 10^{22} to 10^{24} stars in the universe, no other kind of significant life may exist. When you factor in the conditions necessary to create intelligent life, it diminishes the probability much further. The star must be a certain type; the distance from the planet to the star must be within a narrow range. It must have a single moon of a certain size and distance from the planet. In addition, the planet must have a tilt about the star within a certain range. The planet must have a certain composition and must have tectonic plates that collide at just the right times. It must have an atmosphere within a tight range of our planet and the list goes on, including the fact you need another planet of Jupiter's size and an asteroid belt, which needs another planet like Mars between the habitable planet and the Jupiter-sized planet to help in the asteroid creation process. Then, if we factor in what we know of the stars and galaxies, our net result is the relative impossibility of other intelligent life forms in the universe.

"But first, we had to confirm our computer-programmed scenarios worked. It took us a lot of time in the first phase to get any life at all to form, then in the second phase, to get intelligent life to form. In the final phase, we had to delete, replace, and modify each factor to find out how many were crucial and calculate the probability that there could be somewhere else in the universe that this could happen again. I feel, after looking at the data, it's virtually impossible, and that's some feat."

"That's why we should celebrate," cut in the physicist.

And celebrate what they did.

"It's time to open the envelope," the physicist said loudly after about ninety minutes of the group talking happily about how they could present their findings to the world. "Troy will go last," she added. She reached into her pocket, pulled out the packet, broke the seal, and spread out the bets on a table.

The mathematician opened his envelope. He looked at the physicist and said, "I'd like you to work on a project I will be starting in about two months for two hours a day until it is completed. Of course, those are weekdays minus the holidays." Then he looked at the geologist. "I'd like you to make a $50,000 donation to the project I'll be working on." The other two said what they had wanted if they had won.

The physicist opened her envelope and said that she would have wanted the mathematician to work with her on a project too, full-time for three months. The geologist responded that he had asked for help on a project also, for two months.

"Well, I guess I lost," the physicist lamented, her head hanging low, as she picked up Troy's envelope and handed it to him. "Here's your envelope, go ahead and read out what you want me to do."

Troy opened his envelope. He first looked at the geologist and announced "I am working on a project where I can use some help. I had put down full time for two months." The geologist replied that he had asked for $75,000, so he and his wife could go on a nice vacation somewhere and pay down the mortgage. He looked very disappointed, especially since he would be paying out $50,000.

Troy then looked at the physicist and paused for several seconds as he was unsure of himself, then announced in a shaky voice. "My bet is for you to have me over for 50 gourmet meals."

She jumped out of her chair. "Is that all?" she shouted in surprise.

"I love your cooking . . . I thought 50 suppers would have been a lot for you."

"Yes, it takes a little time to prepare but it isn't much bother. I like to cook," she responded, as she sat down again.

"Oh, okay, I guess I should have asked for a 100. Although, what about the poor company?"

"What do you mean poor company?" she said a little shocked.

"Well, I'm not exactly a super-social person, particularly with women."

"Okay, so maybe I should say what I wanted from you." She opened her slip of paper again and added coyly, "My bet was for you to marry me."

"What? Marry you! Are you crazy?" Troy asked, stunned.

"What do you mean?" she answered a little surprised. "Is there something wrong with me? We've been going out at least once a week during this project. It's as if I don't exist. I could take my clothes off and you wouldn't notice."

"Well, probably not," he snickered, "but it's what I said earlier – I'm no Casanova."

She smiled and looked at him intensely, "Maybe I'm desperate then," she said more softly.

He blushed a little. The silence in the room was deafening. He did not think he was ready for this. So far, he had kept his distance from her, other than the odd friendly night out, or to share work projects from time to time. He stared at her for what seemed forever. Then, in case she had changed her mind since the time she had written the bet, he blurted, "I will."

"Will what?" she perked up.

"Marry you."

"Now, I need to know why?" she asked with interest.

"Firstly, because I could probably get more than fifty home-cooked meals that way." Everyone in the room snickered. "And I've grown quite fond of you, especially by working with you on this project. I didn't think you were interested in me, at least not that way."

"'Quite fond' . . . What do you mean by that? It sounds as if you're talking about cats or dogs."

"Oh . . . how about 'like'?" Then he smiled.

"Still too vague, how about stepping it up a bit? I don't want to marry a person who likes me. We've known each other for over three years now."

"I've always kept my relationships with my colleagues strictly platonic."

"I don't want platonic. That's been the problem. You've got platonic on the brain."

"We're in here with several others." He was getting a little embarrassed about their public conversation. "Until we're married, we should maintain professionalism. We can keep the deplatonification process for after the vows. Why did you have to set up this ruse?"

"Yes, I arranged this, although the project took longer than I had hoped. It turned out to be a long time to wait. I was quite certain I would get you to marry me whether I lost or won. If I lost, what happened now would happen. That's why I suggested the losers reveal what their bid was. You would know what my intentions were. If I won, you'd hear what I wanted you to do and you probably would have married me. It was obvious you have a slow pick-up of the attention of a woman, a little dumb, I guess. I also didn't want to just come out and tell you, maybe I'm a little too old-fashioned, I guess, and wanted to make it a little fun. To succeed, I had to take the opposite position to you."

"Well, now that you said you set this up and it was a trick, maybe I should change my mind."

"I don't think you will. I have witnesses here that you said you would, and I didn't even ask you to ask me," she replied in a huff.

"I haven't given you a ring."

"I'm sure you'll correct that deficiency tomorrow in a more formal proposal." She smiled immensely as he played into her hands. The rest of the people in the room were just quietly enjoying the show.

She added, "I'm willing to go with you to the jeweller's so you can get my ring size and I can be sure I get something I like."

"Wait a minute here, who won the bet anyway?" he asked.

"You did, of course. You'll get your fifty home-cooked meals. If you stick with me, I'll give you many more meals like that. Although, you should realise I don't spend every day cooking gourmet meals. I expect to be taken out regularly and cook just regular stuff too, although anything I

142

cook will be much better than the meals I've endured at your place."

Now it was his turn to hide a smile, embarrassed.

Then she added proudly, "and . . . your biggest prize is . . . you get me." She opened her arms and bowed gracefully.

The room erupted in hysterical laughter.

When it quieted down, she added, "I hope you like kids."

"Yes, why?"

"I love kids and want to have a large family," she said firmly.

"What do you mean by large?" he queried.

"Straight away, the first day of marriage, I'm going to get you working on building it. I think a dozen is a good start."

The audience laughed heartily, while Troy sat, beet red, wondering what he had gotten into.

Except for this island circling a rather nondescript star in the Milky Way galaxy, maybe the universe was very likely devoid of other intelligent life but there was lots of life on this world and even more for Troy.

DREAM SCANNER

I present another 1995 story about an engineer who develops a new apparatus that can explain your dreams, or maybe too much. I first wrote this as a two-page story. It evolved significantly since then. Oh, what you can do with your fingers?

Bill was born into poverty and was sickly at birth. Although he had taken some university courses, he did not get high marks. He obtained a bachelor's degree in science with a major in physics and a minor in mathematics then a degree in electrical engineering. He also took courses in chemistry, computer programming, and biology.

He had held several engineering jobs in his passion, designing new products, except for the most part, they were impractical articles that did not meet the requirements of his clients. For the last few years, he had worked as an independent inventor but only one or two of his inventions had turned a profit. He was also a lone wolf, unsociable and uncomfortable in the presence of other people.

Bill's latest passion was an invention he called a dream scanner. He had spent all the money he had in drawing up the schematics and gathering most of the myriad parts he needed to procure before he could start assembly.

He had now decided to solicit some financial help from Jim, his only sibling, who had invested in some of his past inventions. Jim was three years younger and in many ways his opposite. He went into business after secondary school and traded and sold articles that were useful and profitable. He was a builder and investor. His interests were pleasing his clients and making a profit. Jim was much more sociable and had a wife and three children.

Bill invited Jim to his little two-bedroom bungalow for discussions.

Bill heard the slam of a car door in his driveway and walked to the front of the house to pull his door open to welcome Jim in.

"Hi, Jim, thanks for coming this evening. Come and join me in the kitchen and I'll get you a beer," Bill said graciously, as he closed the door and walked with his brother to a chair beside a table.

"Thanks, I can use one," Jim sighed. "I've had a busy and difficult day. The almost $3,000,000 business deal I've been working on has fallen through."

"Sorry to hear that."

"So, what's up with you? How's that brain thingy you started working on a few months ago going?"

"It's a dream scanner and it's going okay. I've developed a plan and started buying some of the parts and equipment I need. Some of the stuff is particular to this task and difficult to get. Some other parts I've been making to try to keep costs down but I've run out of money. I've poured my life savings into this project."

"I didn't know you had any savings," Jim said, almost condescendingly, as he realised Bill's intentions, although he had had his suspicions from the time, he got the invitation.

"I didn't have much but it's gone. I need enough money to buy the rest of the parts so I can start testing," Bill pleaded.

"Even though you're my brother, I can't just keep giving you money. Many of your inventions either have not done what you intended or ended up as impractical items most people wouldn't buy. What's this new thing supposed to do anyway?" Jim enquired.

"It scans dreams."

"How do you scan a dream?"

"Easily; my invention transfers your dreams from your subconscious to your conscious mind so you can recall everything you dreamed about."

"So?" Jim enquired with some doubt.

"So, what do you mean 'So'? This could revolutionise the world." Bill was getting frustrated.

"How?" his brother retorted with a puzzled look on his face.

"Some of my other inventions have done well."

"Big deal, you've made a few bucks on some of them. They were nothing to revolutionise the world. You're starving on what you've made."

"But that'll be my greatest invention yet – the ultimate. This'll tower over what I've done in the past."

"That wouldn't be much of a feat."

"I knew I would come up with something great someday. It's the invention I've been toiling for, living for; my great contribution to humanity. It's so important to the world that I don't want anyone else but you to know about it, so please don't tell anyone about this. I don't want to announce this too soon. I want to build and test it first without interference from anyone."

"You don't even know if it'll work."

"On the contrary, I'm very certain. The concept is sound. You know the brain is very compartmentalised, for example, one section of it takes in the images from your eyes and another part analyses the information. It's the same for all the other senses. There are sections where our emotions are located, as well as areas that deal with our unconscious and conscious thoughts. My invention will create a direct connection between the subconscious and conscious parts of the brain.

"My theory is the unconscious state links to memories of all our experiences which are stored in our brain and our DNA. For example, baby birds, when they become adults, will know where to migrate during the winter even though they've never been there before. I think it may be through a type of communal link that connects all life past, present, and future.

"Also, it may explain why a child, who knows nothing about terror and monsters, will awaken in the middle of the night afraid of something that might just be incomprehensible visions of the past or future it fears.

"My invention may explain how people can predict the future or be inspired by art, or invention. They may not recall the dream, only the inspiration. It would also explain how mediums can connect you to your ancestors."

"The key to the past and future, huh? That sounds very farfetched to me. What you're saying is Thomas Edison didn't invent the light bulb through inspiration but from a scene of a light bulb from the future he saw during a dream. How is this thingamajig supposed to work?"

"I'm going to create a cap with electrodes that will connect the appropriate parts of the brain. I'll be working with a professor at the university with a specialisation in the brain to determine the exact connection sites and how to do it. Then, I'll be ready to set up my device."

"Well, I can't spare much money, especially not for something few people would buy. It may only have a few limited medical applications."

In the end, Jim offered Bill $50,000, which, with all the money from the royalties Bill was receiving for his other inventions, was enough to buy the final components over three years.

During that time, Bill conducted experiments on animals with a university researcher on the appropriate sites in the brain for implanting the electrodes. They had even developed a way to trigger the connection through the skull rather than having to cut it open to insert electrodes. That improvement made the device much simpler and faster to attach the cap and eliminate the risk of infection.

Of course, he did not tell the professor exactly what his invention was but many of Bill's ideas greatly aided the professor with his work.

When he finally finished his device, he stood back to admire it. After considering his options, he decided he would be the best person to test it because of his fear of someone finding out about his invention, and he would be the most able to document the experimental details, the sensations experienced, the adjustments necessary, and the precise details of the results obtained.

Bill proudly invited his brother over to see his dream scanner. The basement of his house contained the bulk of the electronics consisting of seven high-speed computers hooked into a network with lots of random-access memory and terabytes of disk storage. In his attached garage was another computer connected to the others through cables passing through the wall between the basement and garage.

Beside that were a plastic chaise lounge, and a cap that fit on the subject's head wirelessly, to keep it as light and comfortable as possible. There was also a video camera, and a lighting and sound system pointed at the chair to record the events.

"Well, what do you think?" Bill proudly asked his brother.

"It does look impressive with all these wires and other components. I also see you economised well by using a plastic outdoor recliner rather than an upholstered recliner for your victim's testing. Is he or she going to be comfortable enough?"

"Don't mock me."

"I'm not trying to do that but I'm worried about all of this. Have you done adequate animal testing? I see this helmet has a bunch of probes inside it which, I guess, connects to someone's head. Is there a chance you could electrocute someone?"

"The voltage is quite low. As I said before, electronics are just a conduit from certain sections of the brain to others. I earlier used animals to determine the proper voltage and amperage to get the best results."

"Who are you going to use as a test subject?"

"Me. I need someone with a scientific mind to report the results thoroughly."

"What! Aren't you nervous about being the Guinee pig?" Jim asked incredulously.

"Not really."

"Will there be any adverse effects?"

"None, I'm aware of right now. I'm not worried. We didn't have problems with our animal testing."

"That's reassuring!" Jim said doubtfully. "Is there any risk involved?"

"Of course, but no advance in science is without risk. Here, the risk is small but the gain is immense."

"I don't like your conducting the experiments on yourself. There will be nobody to monitor you while you're under the influence of the equipment."

"Don't worry about me. I plan to take all necessary precautions. I've already had myself scanned for the probe settings specific to me with the assistance of the university professor."

"I insist a doctor or someone else qualified be here to monitor you during the test."

"I don't want anyone and can't pay for anyone."

"I'll pay someone to be here."

"No, I can't let anyone know I have something like this."

Jim paused for several seconds as he thought of something else that he could say. Finally, he offered, "Look, I'm willing to be here with you. At least, I'd be here if you needed me."

"Please, Jim, just let me follow my dream. This is my project and I'd like to run it as I think is best. You know you won't have time to be away from your family. Please just let me be. I'm very confident of success."

Uneasily, Jim left saying, "Well, good luck, Bro. Call me after the test."

The next day, all the equipment was set up. He divided his probe strength scale into ten levels and set it to one. He checked the probes and the electronics. He strapped himself into the chair and fastened the cap onto his head, so it would not move.

He felt lightheaded after he flipped the switch and the connection made. He began to drift to sleep. His mind blanked out then his face suddenly lit up with a smile. He was asleep he realised but it was as if he were awake and aware of everything going on. It was a wonderful sensation.

As he lay on the recliner, thoughts were filling his head. Numbers and letters floated by. Suddenly, he recognised a formula that soon transfigured into another one, the formula for the theory of everything physicists have been seeking for years – how gravity and all the other forces link into one unified theory. There were also many other confusing ideas. Then he blanked out into a type of unconsciousness he thought was just another form of sleep.

Suddenly, things got wild in his head. He was back at the home of his youth as a little boy with his mother and father. He was learning to walk and was using the walls as his support. He kept leaning his hands on the walls as he travelled around the house. Finally, his mother picked him up put him into his high chair and fed him. Then, that too disappeared into blackness.

When he awoke, he felt relaxed but his mind contained so much information that he spent the next three days making verbal notes into his computer. It was unusual for him to remember so much information in such detail. He was very excited about the early results he was getting. However, because of his insecurity about someone finding out about his device, he encrypted and pass-worded all his system files and records, and obtained software to prevent anyone from trying to break into his computer system.

When he had finally completed his notes, he prepared his equipment and himself for the next test. He lay down on the chair, placed the cap on his head again, turned the control to the next higher level and turned it on.

At first, there was not much more than what he had seen during the first session. Then a familiar formula popped up then transformed. This excited him immensely, as it was a refinement of Einstein's work, which would allow faster-than-light travel. It was so simple he wondered why no one had thought of it before. Other formulae he did not understand were swarming in his head. After a few minutes, that phase ended.

Similar, to the first test, the second phase began with his riding a horse. This time, he was racing through a grassy field with hundreds of other men. He held a sword high in the air and front of him was another group of men with banners flying high charging towards him. Soon, the opponents clashed with swords cutting deeply in a furious attack. It seemed to go on for some time as the battle ebbed and flowed. The events he was experiencing made him feel the exhaustion of the rider as he fought for his life. The opponent slashed him several times and he was in pain. Finally, the battle was over. He, and a few of his remaining colleagues, were victoriously holding their weapons high in the air over their heads in victory. He blanked into sleep again.

When he awoke, he did not feel rested but felt pain in his arms and back. His muscles must have tensed in response to the battle fought during his dream.

While recording his experiences, he puzzled over why he did not comprehend the other floating concepts he saw. He understood Einstein's theory and, when he saw it in the dream, he could spot how it led to the next level. He decided to spend a few days researching a few new math and physics concepts before he went into the next dream session.

As soon as he was ready, he lay down on the chair again and turned the knob to the next level. During the concept phase, two or three more formulae made sense. This confirmed that he could only make sense of any concept and its further refinement if he already had enough knowledge and understanding of the base formulae in advance.

During the event phase this time, there seemed to be many different scenes going on at the same time. However, he eventually focused on one where he was, like the last time, on a horse. He was clad in armour and held a large pole while riding quickly toward another person on a horse. With a few lithe moves, he outmanoeuvred the other person and knocked him off his horse. The people standing close by waved and cheered.

So, it went to the next level. First, the concepts swirled before him then he experienced past or future events. The higher he set the dial, the further into the past, or future, were the events he experienced. He even repeated a power level a few times and found the experiences varied each time. This would permit historians to study the past at different points in time while remaining at the same level.

He also confirmed that he experienced only events of the males of his family line, so different people would have different experiences. His device really would be a marvel for humanity. He was starting to see a Nobel Prize in his future.

By level eight, he was having multiple event experiences in his dreams. He was going further into the past or future. At one point, he had seemingly experienced the dawn of man. Twice, he had pictured himself as an ape-like being foraging through the jungle with his ape-like companions.

He also found that the increase in levels was having a greater effect on him; he was more tired when he awoke, and he was having dream sessions during normal sleep between uses of the device.

Bill rested for three weeks before he prepared for level nine. He wanted to complete his notes and study some more concepts in mathematics, physics, and chemistry, as well as take some time for the extraneous dreaming to diminish.

At level nine, the concept sequence was intense. It jolted him. The added research before this session resulted in more comprehension of the formulae swimming in front of his eyes, with more new revelations in science.

The events phase had now become a swirling eddy of past and future flashes. The first one he picked out was during the Middle Ages and lasted several minutes. The best he could make out from the next one, he was an unidentifiable animal, probably four-footed, foraging for food. The third was a scene from the future where there were no roads. Cars spanned the skies guided by satellite and computers; all one had to do was get in the vehicle, tell it where you wanted to go, and off you went with no intervention on the part of the driver at all. One more vision from the past was of his mother shortly before she died. Bill relived the experience of her death and he cried profusely. He entered another period of dreaming but panicked and struggled to pull himself out of sleep so he could shut off the unit before he could go through the sequence again. He removed his cap and lay there a few minutes, stunned.

He looked at the chronometer. He had been on the device for almost ninety minutes. The excessive number of events had alerted him to the fact he had been on the device too long.

He fell into a deep, exhausted sleep. When he woke up, he recalled more dreams he had had without the use of the machine. After this session, he rested for almost a month while he recorded everything that he had experienced.

He had found in the earlier sessions he could leave the unit on throughout the sleep period and he would wake up before sixty minutes had passed. With each level, it was becoming more difficult to get out of the sleep state. He had always conducted the experiments after an afternoon nap to keep the sleep state short. Because of his experience at level nine, he built a timer to have the session automatically shut down after sixty minutes. He did two more sessions at level nine with the timer in operation to ensure the timing mechanism worked.

Throughout the process, Bill communicated regularly with his brother by telephone. By now, Jim's curiosity had increased to such an extent he urged his brother to meet him for supper at a restaurant.

At the restaurant, they discussed how things were going with Jim and his family but the conversation soon drifted to Bill and his work.

"So how is it going with your gizmo?" Jim asked teasingly.

Bill suddenly looked around nervously but it was a quiet night at the restaurant and no one was close enough to their table to hear their conversation. He relaxed a bit and corrected Bill in a whisper. "It's a dream scanner."

"Whatever," Jim replied, also quietly, trying not to sound too interested in his brother's pet project, while preserving Bill's need for secrecy.

"It's going okay."

"Only, okay? Over the past few months, you've sounded very excited about what you're finding. You've said you're travelling back in time and going into the future."

"Not exactly, a better explanation would be to say I've found a genetic trail going forward and backwards in time."

"Hum, interesting . . . and it's something like a family line."

"Exactly, my 'gizmo', as you call it, permits me to amplify my subconscious connection to this trail, so I can experience my ancestors' and progenies' life experiences along it. So far, I can see back as far as what seems to be the dawn of the mammal and for some distance into the future."

"Wow, I can see why you're so immersed in your work. You may be onto something."

"This is what I predicted at our first meeting about the scanner," Bill affirmed proudly. "Also, recall our recent telephone conversation that, in the first phase of the dream, I can connect to our collective intellect, so I can see all we've learned and will ever learn. I can understand it though, only if I have enough knowledge to comprehend its significance.

Right now, I've amassed enough knowledge to write many publishable articles in major scientific periodicals or write numerous theses, or many breakthrough articles that would permit us to travel through space and more. If a medical researcher hooked up to this device, I believe he or she would learn of cures for cancer and other diseases. A surgeon would learn new revolutionary techniques in surgery."

Jim sat dumbfounded. If what Bill was saying was true, he had invented a valuable tool for humanity, and perhaps the greatest device ever created. Bill was bubbling with enthusiasm and he could see why. He could also see why Bill had wanted to keep it so secret to ensure he maintained ownership but Jim could also see a sinister side. In the wrong hands, this device could be dangerous but then, Bill had not described 'seeing' anything sinister in the future. Surely some disaster caused by this scanner would have been noteworthy enough to notice in his sessions, unless it occurred further into the future than he could experience at this point in his experiments.

Jim felt proud of his brother and his achievements. The man he had formerly almost scorned had risen in stature immensely. "Wow, all I can say is, wow," Jim blurted. "Have you almost completed your research?"

"Getting close."

"What are you going to do when you're done?"

"I don't know yet. I don't know if I should use my notes to write my scientific discoveries to take advantage of my work to this point, announce my invention outright, or wait until I get the patenting process started."

"When you're done, let's have a little celebration – on me, and we can discuss your thoughts. I'm interested in seeing this completed and I'll help in whatever way I can.

"I'm puzzled about something in your theory, though. You said you could see past and future events through your family line?"

"Yes, it seems so from the evidence I have received to this point and the knowledge I have obtained through the device."

"If that's true, then how could you have seen the future? Now, you have no family line into the future, unless because I'm your brother, you can see through mine, or you still have a chance for love. You're not that old."

Bill stood stunned by his brother's observation. He had not thought of that. Suddenly, he turned beet red.

Jim noticed the colour change. "What's the matter?"

He stammered, "You're right. I hadn't thought about it . . . It's been a long time, a very long time . . ." Bill continued.

"A long time for what?" Jim looked, puzzled.

"In my third year of university, I met this young lady who . . . for some reason . . . was crazy about me."

"My God, and you never told me!" Jim retorted incredulously.

"I tried to stay away from her, as I was focussed on my studies. . but I did go out on a couple of dates with her and one evening in her residence she just threw herself at me and before I knew it. It was only once . . ."

"I guess that's all you need," Jim said in disbelief.

"Well, anyway . . . Father would have been furious about it and I was not interested in getting married. Maybe she thought that having a baby would convince me to marry her. I don't know. In the end, she decided to keep the baby. Her parents helped and supported her. They moved out of town a year later and I never saw them again. I did get to see the little tyke, named David, a couple of times before they moved."

"Well . . . my brother is a father! You've never told anyone about it. I never knew you had a secret life. Sometimes you're a mystery to me."

"I was embarrassed about all of it. What's to tell?"

"My, my, that closes that loop. I guess I'd never have known that if you hadn't developed that machine of yours. Do you want me to keep that a secret, or can I let my family know they have a cousin somewhere?"

"It doesn't matter. It was a long time ago. By the way, I did find a side effect from the device."

"Oh?"

"For a few days after sessions, I had vivid dreams of all kinds of things, such as what I experienced in a scanner session but the most disturbing of them were of my life.

"I had dreams of when I was very young and how sick I was all the time. Mom was always under great stress because of it. The dreams were a mixed blessing for me, because, although they were so disturbing, I could see how much love Mom had for me. Her love was so endless and her patience so deep. My love and admiration for her grew stronger.

"The most disturbing dreams, though, were of Dad. I had mostly forgotten him but the dreams brought him back in Technicolor. He was so hard on all of us, with his almost excessive puritanical ways. It even drove Mom to distraction. It seemed everything was a sin. Every time we did anything, we got a whipping. It so influenced my life.

"I became afraid of doing anything and withdrew into myself. I lost any self-confidence I may have had. I became almost afraid of women, as I saw them as a source of sin. I had the opportunity perhaps for some love and I ran away from it. That woman at university may have been the person I needed. The dreams I had of her were so pleasant, I could feel the love she had but never realised it at the time. For you, it was the opposite; you worked around Dad and it made you stronger but the dreams of Dad made me see myself for who I am and made me understand myself better.

"I also dreamed of all the horrible experiences I had at school. It didn't help that I was sick often but I repressed the other students' bullying so deeply that I forgot how bad they were. I was the target of every joke and harassment. They beat, burned, insulted, demeaned, and embarrassed me, particularly the day they pulled off my pants and I had to run to the teacher naked to try to get my pants back. The teachers seemed not to care. The policy seemed to be that bullying made you stronger. It puts hair on your chest. Teachers expected kids to solve their problems and fight their own battles.

"It was hard to see any benefit I got from experiencing those dreams, except for your part in them. Even though you were three years younger, you stood up for me. When you started school, the bullying reduced somewhat, except when you weren't around. Those events made you tough because you learned to fight older kids. You got your bruises but you didn't care because you were my brother. I'd forgotten most of that part too, so I learned from those dreams what a special person you have been in my life, the love I got from you, and all the fun experiences we had.

"Furthermore, I dreamed of university and my scraping by, then my workplace experiences. I must have been so strange to everyone. I wouldn't talk to people. I was in a world of my own. I think some of them tried to work with me but others didn't bother.

"So here I am – a relative recluse. The only person I think who may have seen anything in me is somewhere else in the world looking after my son. I wonder if I should try to find her after I get this testing completed, although she has probably long ago married someone else.

"So, over the last few months, I have done more than my fair share of crying – a grown man crying but it helped to release a lot of pent-up emotions that have been repressed all these years. So, it was a double-edged side-effect of my dream scanner. I've had a lot of reflection time."

He delivered it as a soliloquy. Bill had stared at a point on the wall perpendicular to his brother's location and ignored his presence. His eyes finally turned to look at Jim, whose eyes were red and puffy. A pile of tissues was sitting on his dinner plate.

Jim, at first, said nothing. He was trying to get over the intense emotions he had felt while he listened to his brother speak. Then he said, "You brought so many memories back to me. I remembered the battles I had with Dad and the fights at school. I was constantly getting into trouble because of them. I hated school so much that I just went out and got a job when school was over. It was sobering to hear your trials and how they blended with mine." The compassion he felt for his brother made him feel much closer to him than he had ever felt before.

Supper ended and the conversations were completed, so Jim paid the restaurant bill. For the first time, they put their arms around each other and patted each other's backs before they parted.

For the next two days, both brothers recovered from their meeting but they both re-energised to get back to work.

Jim was now considering the marketing options for this potential new product. Certainly, the research world would love to probe the usefulness of this product but other scientists of all domains would have another useful tool for research and invention. Psychiatrists may be able to use it as a tool in their work. Historians would love it. He was not sure yet if it would have practical consumer-level application but he would have to check it out himself to see what was possible in that area. He now had the same level of enthusiasm for the device as his brother.

After a four-week break to finish his notes and prepare, Bill lay down on the chair, placed the cap on his head, set the level to ten and turned on the device. First, he grew rigid, as if he were in a catatonic state then frightened, because this was happening much more intensely than any time before. He relaxed when it passed then blacked out briefly. The colours and information that flowed in front of him were amazing. The formulae were the same, as he had not changed his level of knowledge further but when the mangled scenes of past and future events appeared, they were fast and furious. He found he had even more control over what he could see.

From the flashes, he picked out the basic beginning of genes and the genesis of cells. He could confirm now that eukaryotic cells, the cells of plants and animals, had been formed from the gradual inclusion of other, at first symbiotic, prokaryotic cells within another prokaryotic cell to create the nucleus, and eventually the organelles like the mitochondria which provide energy for the cell, and the chloroplasts which convert the sun's energy into food for plant cells. It was amazing how it had occurred over hundreds of millions of years.

He sought out and connected to an early mammal that had seen the asteroid that hit the Earth and brought about the extinction of the dinosaurs. He found the first biped, the first father of humanity, the missing link and could feel the new power of his intellect. He sought, then felt the power of the mind of the first Homo sapiens, whose aggression and greed would wipe out all the other human-like competitors to become the most dominant animal on the planet. He linked to one of the last men on Earth and saw through his progeny's eyes and sensed through his brain the end of man's dominion over the world. He was proud his final successor had made it that far.

There was just so much to see, so much to choose from and he knew he had less than thirty minutes left to see what else there was to experience in that session. He was seeing so much so quickly it was overpowering.

Something else had swirled before him several times already that piqued his interest but it seemed somewhat elusive. He searched for it. His curiosity aroused but it continued to escape his grasp until he finally began to pull it into focus. As it began to gel, he realised there was an afterlife, as this appeared to be the collective essence of all life, living and dead. Time was disappearing. What he found was not a visible vapour trail but a trail of no time, where everything stopped and everything was moving, where he saw birth and death, the beginning, and the end. What he saw was so bright it was blinding, and now, instead of being elusive, it seemed to be pulling him in.

Suddenly, a woman appeared out of the brightness and approached him. At first, he did not recognise her but as she got closer, he was shocked.

He called out, "Mother, is that you?"

"Yes, Billy," was the reply.

"I'm in a dream and can see the future, right?"

"Son, the time has disappeared. There is no time here."

She approached him and embraced him in her arms.

"The timer on the computer will soon terminate this session but it is so nice to see you," he said, sobbing.

He gave his mother a firm hug. It was such a warm and comforting feeling. He began to cry softly, as he still missed his mother after all the years since she died. He remembered all the pains and suffering of his life. The arms of his mother were wiping them away and he felt such peace.

"You don't have to leave Billy, just stay with me. You can be hurt no more."

The light swallowed him up. He knew now that he had obtained the ultimate truth, the truth that tied all the laws of physics, mathematics, chemistry, biology, and philosophy together into one – there is a God.

* * *

Jim had not heard from his brother for two days. He had called Bill several times by telephone, with no response. That had never happened before. With the spare key to the house Bill had given to him many years ago, he drove over and rang the doorbell. After he received no response, he unlocked the door and entered the house and then the garage. He looked at the lifeless form strapped to the chair and called the police.

He returned to the body of his brother and stared. Somehow Bill looked unfamiliar. He could not describe the change but Bill looked more at peace than he had ever seen him. It seemed strange but Bill's face appeared to be smiling. He knew Bill was dead and yet he looked so alive. The doorbell interrupted his hypnotic state.

Two uniformed officers were standing in the doorway. He invited them in. They asked for his side of the story and he told them. The police asked to see the basement of the house and the garage.

When they arrived inside the garage, Jim said, "I came in and this is what I found."

"Did you touch anything?" one of the officers asked.

"No, sir, I left everything as it was."

The police communicated with their headquarters to report what they had seen.

The detective at headquarters said they would be over to take over the investigation.

About 40 minutes later, a team of three detectives arrived. They talked first with the uniformed officers, who left shortly after the conversation ended. One of the three remaining officers began to take photographs of the scene, while the other two interviewed Jim. They looked over the scene and took notes. They asked him if he knew the passwords to the computers or where Bill may have kept a record of them. When he said he could not help them, they suggested Jim could return home as they would be there for some time. They recommended that he be available for further questioning if required.

Jim left the key to the house with the officers and left.

Several days later he got a call from one of the investigating officers for him to come to the station to pick up his key and have a chat with him. At the meeting, the officer told him the investigation ended. They had concluded there was no evidence of foul play. The autopsy had indicated his brother had died of coronary arrest, although there was no evidence that he had had any pre-existing health problem that could have caused it. The presumption was that something transpired between him and the device to which he was connected.

He also said they had taken the computer in the garage and two from the basement to their laboratory for analysis. They had been trying to boot them up to find out if there had been a malfunction of the equipment to cause the death but they had not been able to get into them. They had started a routine to crack the password of the one in the garage, but, at one point, their attempt to get in had caused another routine to run to destroy the files. They had stopped the routine before it had done much damage to them. The officer then returned the house key and said that they would release his brother's body for burial. They had also returned the computers to the house.

Jim returned home to the calm of his family. He had been distraught throughout the investigations. He had wondered if there was anything that he could have done to prevent what had happened but there was likely no way he could have stopped Bill from continuing with the experiments.

Most of his spare time for the next few days was making funeral arrangements and attending the burial. By searching through Bill's records, Jim found his brother's Will which left all his property to Jim. He spent more time with the issues associated with that. He settled Bill's debts and slowly sold off, gave away, or threw out most of Bill's belongings, except for the house and the scanner. He found no sign of passwords, or any information to help him in his quest to learn more about the scanner. He even searched Bill's attic and around the yard.

Once he had time to clear his head of all that had happened, he thought, he would try to salvage what he could of Bill's work and hire an expert technologist to look at the equipment. Bill had worked so hard and put so much of himself into the scanner it had become a part of him. He was convinced the scanner could have won Bill a Nobel Prize.

Jim convinced a computer engineer he knew to examine the scanner. The engineer asked him many questions about his brother to give him clues as to what simple passwords he might have used. For two days, he worked on the equipment but found no way to crack the security system. He told Jim there might be ways to read the drives directly but it was very expensive to do and might not be fruitful, especially if Bill had encrypted everything.

Bill's desire for secrecy was hindering Jim's efforts to give his brother the renown he deserved. If Bill at least had entrusted him with the passwords to the system, he could have done something to get Bill's work out to the world. His brother's confidence in his invention had made him careless.

Jim moved the equipment to his basement and sold the house. After two months, Bill's wife began pressing him to either store the equipment somewhere else or get rid of it. Jim was reluctant because he sensed Bill's essence was still present in it.

Finally, the time came when he decided he could no longer hold onto the scanner. He dismantled it, put the hard drives aside and took the metal to a recycler. The rest he threw away. The engineer properly destroyed the hard drives to ensure no one would ever be able to recover anything from them.

When the destruction was complete, Jim felt a profound loss. Just as the two brothers had developed a closer bond, Bill was gone. He took a few days off from work and stayed by Bill's tomb for hours, hanging his head in tears and remorse remembering the hard life his brother had endured. As he missed his brother, he also felt profound sorrow for the great loss of the dream scanner. He would never know for certain if Bill's invention would have been the panacea his brother had predicted.

It was late in the day and the sun was dipping below the horizon. It was getting dark. The long shadows extending from the gravestones made the site look eerie. He looked up at the sky to note that some of the stars were becoming visible; then it struck him. When he was a little boy, his grandfather had died and he had talked about death with his mother. Why he was thinking of it now puzzled him. He had long forgotten about it. They had been out in the yard at about the same time of day and she had told him that everyone who died became a new star in the sky.

It seemed very childish to him now but a star seemed to flash at him. It may have been the impending darkness had only made it more visible than before, however, he suddenly smiled and a few tears trickled from his eyes. He remembered the look of his brother's face, with that soft smile, lying dead on his chair that day in the house, and how strange it looked. To him, it seemed as if the face glowed.

He pulled out a tissue and wiped his eyes. He looked back at the star and winked at it and could have sworn it had winked back. He smiled again, comforted. He was ready to go home and to life.

JUDGE

I woke up one morning in the summer of 2010 with a new story idea – how I love inspiration! How to present the story came a couple of months later. It is about judgement perhaps in the future. I hope you like this and it shakes you up.

"Mam, youse supposa ge' up now."

Marie opened her eyes and looked up at the figure bent over her, then over at her clock. It was seven o'clock and indeed time to get up.

She sneered at the figure and ordered, "Get our breakfast ready."

She got up, had her shower, and dressed. She got her daughter out of bed. She went downstairs to the smell of bacon and eggs with coffee. She sat down at the table. The figure brought her a full plate and cup, which she sniffed with relish.

"Damn you, you know I like my bacon crisper than this, and the coffee is hardly warm. How many times must I tell you? I should replace you. I don't know why I keep you around. Now fry the bacon a little longer and zap the coffee, and do it quickly so the eggs will still be hot, and bring me some pepper."

Marie's slave sulkily did as she said then brought the plate and cup back to her.

"Now, remember how it should be for the next time, you idiot," she said angrily.

Her daughter walked into the kitchen, gently hugged her mother's neck, and sat down. The slave brought her a bowl of cornflakes, a glass of milk, and two slices of buttered toast. Marie looked at the food and said to her slave, "At least you got that right."

They finished their meals and washed up. As she had a day off school, Marie's daughter would be going to work with her mother.

Marie gathered her files for work. At eight hours and fifteen minutes, they left the house and walked to the public transit stop, which consisted of two signs, one for people and the other for slaves. They were the only ones at her stop but there were three slaves huddled at theirs. When the bus arrived, they got on the front section of it and the others got on the back. There was a Plexiglas wall between the two halves of the bus to prevent contact between people and slaves. When they got to the stop closest to her workplace, they got off and were soon climbing the stairs to her building.

The security system recognised Marie and she entered the building with her daughter. They walked down a hall, climbed a flight of stairs, and entered her beautifully decorated office, which had a huge desk and plush chair.

She had worked hard to achieve this. She studied law, articled, and was called to the bar twenty years ago. After seventeen years as an exceptional lawyer, she became a judge. She was proud of her accomplishments.

In the morning, her daughter wanted to stay in her mother's office to read one of her textbooks. Marie suggested she watch the afternoon session of her court. Marie sat down in her chair and pored over her case files for the day. As usual, almost all the cases were about issues with slaves. As she scanned through them, she snickered at some and others she gave looks of disgust. Finally, she glanced at the only person's file and just shook her head.

The morning sessions seemed so long and tedious. In three cases, she ordered the death penalty, while in others she handed down prison sentences, corporal punishments, or labouring in work-gangs but she dispatched all her judgements quickly and efficiently.

She and her daughter had lunch in the cafeteria and returned to the office. Marie rested awhile and carefully read the file on the only person of the day and only case of the afternoon, as cases for people required more deliberation and consideration.

She led her daughter to the visitor's gallery of her court and entered the courtroom through her office at 13:00 hours. She looked around the courtroom and at the people standing in the gallery who were curious to see what interesting cases may arise. She sat down and everyone followed suit.

The clerk brought the court to order and swore in all the witnesses. Marie stared down at a young lady and older woman behind the defence's table. She looked at a police officer and an older woman at the prosecution table.

The clerk opened, "This is case number 11298346, the state versus Jean Borkowski. I'd like to remind everyone the court's proceedings will be recorded electronically."

The judge looked down at the defendant and said, "Ms. Jean Borkowski, please stand." The young lady at the defence table stood up. "You've been accused of some very serious offences against the New World government, namely: naming a slave, consorting with a slave, and disturbing public order. I see on your notarised response you've pleaded guilty to the first charge but not guilty to the second and third. Are you maintaining the same plea?"

The accused responded, "Yes, your Honour."

"You've also stated you've chosen trial by judge. Do you still wish to proceed with the case in that manner?"

"Yes, your Honour, I do."

"You may be seated."

Jean sat down.

"The prosecution may proceed with the case." Marie liked her proceedings to be simple and clear-cut.

The prosecutor stood up and said, "Your Honour, I'd like to call Constable Smith to the stand."

The police officer rose and took the stand.

The prosecutor opened the case. "Constable Smith, would you please recount what happened on July 12 of this year related to this case."

"Yes. At eight hours and two minutes, Precinct 15 received a call from Fiona McGregor. She informed us the defendant had called her slave by a name and she had patted its head and smiled at it."

There was a gasp in the courtroom.

The officer continued, "I visited the informant at Unit 1125 – 14th Avenue and she did confirm what she had said on the video call. I examined the common wall with the apartment next door to Unit seventeen but there was no sound coming through the wall at that moment. As the defendant was at work for the day, I left.

"I returned to the building at sixteen hours and thirteen minutes of the same day and knocked on the door of Unit 17. The defendant answered it and allowed me entry.

"Inside, I noted the defendant did have a slave in attendance and it served me coffee at the start of my questioning of the defendant. I told her I had received a complaint that she had named her slave. She did admit it. I asked her what name she had given it and she said 'Assert'. I asked her why she had decided to name it and she answered she had gotten tired of calling it 'slave' or 'hey, you' all the time. I asked her if she knew it was illegal to do so and she answered 'Yes'.

"I then asked her if she had also patted it on the head on July twelfth, on or about o eighth hundred hours. She said she was rewarding her slave for a job well done. I repeated my question and she repeated her response.

"I also asked her if she had smiled at her slave at that time. She said she had not smiled at the slave but had smiled because she was happy with what her slave had done. I then arrested the defendant."

"The prosecution has no more questions, your Honour."

The defence lawyer stood up and said, "I have no questions for this witness, your Honour," and sat down.

The judge said to the witness, "You may step down."

The police officer returned to the seat at the prosecution table.

The prosecution lawyer then said, "I call my second witness, your Honour, Ms. Fiona McGregor."

Fiona took the stand.

"Now, tell me, Ms. McGregor, when did you hear the defendant call her slave a name?"

"Three times. I heard her call it by name through the wall next to her apartment. I heard it on the 13th of June, sometime in the morning, just before she left for work. I think it was just after eight. I heard it again on July eighth in the evening around nine. I heard her address it by a name a third time, July twelfth, when I was leaving my apartment to collect my newspaper. Jean had opened her door to leave and I overheard her say goodbye to her slave and call it by name."

"What name did she call it?"

"Assert."

"What else did she do?"

"I saw her pat it on the head and smile at it."

There was another gasp in the courtroom.

The judge asked for quiet and told the people in the gallery that if anyone else disturbed the court, they would have to leave.

"I have no further questions, your Honour."

The prosecutor sat down.

The defence attorney stood, stepped out from behind the table, and approached the witness.

"Ms. McGregor, how clearly can you hear through Ms. Borkowski's wall?"

"Quite well; the building is old and lets the sound through quite easily."

"Could it be an error as to what you heard through it?"

"No, but I didn't want to notify the police the first two times until I was sure. That is why I waited until I heard her in an open place. I just confirmed what I had heard earlier." Fiona knew what the penalties were for not reporting a crime and this was a good excuse for not having reported it earlier.

"On the morning of July twelfth, where on the head did Ms. Borkowski pat the slave?"

"It was in the front middle of its head, like this." She demonstrated the pat with her hand on her head.

"Can you demonstrate the exact type of smile Ms. Borkowski used on her face that morning?"

"It was like this." She demonstrated it with her face.

"Are you sure it appeared like that?" The lawyer was trying to determine if it looked more like a sneer than a smile of fondness, and what she saw was the latter.

"Definitely."

The defence attorney paused for a while then said, "No more questions, your Honour," and headed back to sit down.

The judge instructed, "You may return to your seat."

The prosecutor rose and stated, "I rest my case, your Honour."

The judge looked at the defence table and asked, "Do you have any witnesses for the defence?"

The defence attorney stood and said, "Yes, your Honour. I would like to call Ms. Jean Borkowski to the witness stand.

The young woman at the defence table stepped up to the stand.

"My client has pleaded guilty to the crime of naming her slave, so I will move on to the other two charges."

"Ms. Borkowski, would you explain to me why you patted your slave's head and smiled at it on July 12th?"

"It made my breakfast well and was particularly good that morning. I've found that if you reward your slave for jobs well done, it'll continue to do well and perhaps may want to do even better in the future. I had only one other slave before and it was awful – almost useless – and eventually I had to get rid of it. This one has been so good; I hope I can keep it for as long as I can."

"So, what you are clarifying is you were not smiling at the slave because it performed well but really to yourself because you were feeling happy about the situation you were in. You just happened to be facing the slave at the time.

"Objection, your Honour. This is a leading question," the prosecutor challenged.

"Sustained," the judge said.

"Now, about the patting actions; you are a teacher, are you?" the defence attorney continued.

"Yes, I am – of kindergarten students."

"Do you pat your students' heads or backs?"

"Among other rewards, yes. I find it greatly improves their performance."

"So, it has become an automatic response then to reward in this manner?"

"Yes, I guess, I've forgotten myself a few times with my slave but I find it works so well."

"No more questions, your Honour."

"Does the prosecution wish to cross-examine the accused?" the judge asked.

"Yes, your Honour," the prosecutor responded and stood.

"Ms. Borkowski, you heard the witness for the prosecution. Do you deny you called your slave a name in those other two circumstances?"

"I did it on July 12 but I wouldn't know for sure about the other two times because I don't recall if I had called it a name on those particular days."

"Have you ever called your slave a name before? I should remind you, you're under oath."

"I will not deny it."

"How many times a day have you called it a name?"

"It would depend on the day; maybe some days it would be never, and other times maybe five times or more."

"Thank you, Ms. Borkowski.

"When did you first call your slave a name?"

"I don't recall the date, I guess about six months before July twelfth."

"On July twelfth, did you pat your slave on the head?"

"Yes but . . ."

The prosecutor interrupted her. "Just answer the question, Ms. Borkowski. Had you ever patted its head any time before that day?"

"Not that I recall," she responded, a little flustered.

"How about any other taps, pats, or other contact?"

"I've patted it on the back two or three times."

"And when did you start doing that?"

"About three months ago, or so." Her voice was beginning to quiver.

"Did you smile at your slave on July twelfth?"

"Not really."

"What do you mean by that?"

"I admit I smiled in front of it."

"Okay, have you ever smiled in front of your slave at any other time?"

"Probably, if I'm happy, I smile," she replied matter-of-factly.

"Now, even though ignorance is no excuse for breaking the law, are you aware of the law associated with the offences and were you aware before you were arrested?"

"Yes, I learned about them when I was in high school."

"Didn't you sign an agreement before purchasing your slave that laid out the conditions of ownership?"

"Yes."

"I have here a notarised copy of that agreement with your signature on it. We obtained it as a piece of evidence of your crime. Would you please look at it and confirm that is your signature?"

Ms. Borkowski looked at the document presented to her and affirmed, "Yes, that's my signature."

The prosecutor took it back from her and said, "I am returning to the court Exhibit A, attesting to the fact the defendant purchased the slave and, with her signature, agreed to the conditions of sale as well as affirmed her knowledge of the Acts and Regulations associated with such ownership."

The prosecutor handed the document to the judge, who looked at it and passed it to the court clerk.

"Ms Borkowski, I also have a notarized copy of your psychological assessment before you could buy a slave. You were informed of the results, were you not?"

"Yes, I was," she answered.

"The report said you did not score well on the test. They found you to be low in maturity, given a conditional license to buy a slave for one year, and they monitored you during that time. When you sold back your first slave, the authorities allowed you a new one, which I believe is the one you have at present. Is that correct?"

"Yes, it is," she responded.

"May I present this report as court exhibit B, indicating the defendant was found to be lacking in maturity and was only conditionally allowed to possess a slave? Although the probationary period is over, her rating in this report is relevant to this case, because her actions indicate she appears to lack maturity, which is not a defence for her action but supports the likelihood she could commit the alleged crimes."

The prosecutor handed the report to the judge, who took a few minutes to read it before turning it over to the court clerk.

The prosecutor said, "I have no further questions, your Honour."

"You may step down from the stand, Ms. Borkowski," the judge instructed.

Jean Borkowski stepped down and returned to her chair behind the defence table.

The judge continued, "Does the defence have any other witnesses?"

The defence attorney stepped up.

"Yes, I do, your Honour. I would like to call Ms. Janet Borkowski to the stand."

The older woman behind the defence table got up and took the witness stand.

The defence attorney walked in front of her. "Would you please state your name and relationship to the defendant?"

"My name is Janet Borkowski, and I am her mother."

"You heard your daughter's testimony a few minutes ago. She mentioned she didn't mean to smile at, or pat, her slave because she was naturally inclined to do such actions to young students in her class at school. As her mother, you're probably the one who would know her the most. Would you tell the court what kind of person she is?"

"From the time she was a baby, she was always such a wonderful person. She was always smiling cheerfully. Nothing seemed to disturb her. She got along with everyone. She was so kind. Her loving nature led her to her profession as a teacher, because she loves children so much. I imagine someday she'll have children of her own."

"So, you would not be surprised she would smile in front of her slave?"

"I'd be surprised if she didn't. She is always cognisant of any laws, so I'm sure she smiled because she was happy and not because of any connection to the slave. She told me she had a very intelligent slave that learned quickly and did its job well. She had had such a stupid one before. This one was a breath of fresh air. She was very happy about her life."

"What about this patting business?"

"I'm a little surprised by that but she's also a very physical person. As a teacher, she uses praise a lot. Most of the time it's in the form of gifts of gold stars but often it's a gentle pat on the head or back. As a child, she was afraid of slaves. The two we had when she was young frightened her and she felt nervous around them. She tended to avoid them. Some slaves are very childlike and she may have inadvertently patted it as a form of reward for work done well. It's her nature. I did see her current slave once and I found it quite young, very gentle, and hard-working. She may have pictured it as she would a child and patted it without thinking.

"She loved history and was very knowledgeable about slave history and the importance of adhering to the laws associated with them. I'm certain she would not have intentionally broken any laws. I'm disappointed, however, she would have given one a name." She sighed. "When she was young, she tended to give everything a special name according to what she thought of it. She even gave special names to people. For example, one of her aunts she named 'Ms. Prissy'. Unfortunately, she also named our slaves but they were joke names. One was 'Grumpy' and the other was 'Dopey'. I guess she needed to give her current one a name too but you can see it's not a real name but an attribute. She has even named plants and inanimate things like rocks and dolls. She was always an imaginative child. Since she didn't use actual 'names' in the real sense of the word, they shouldn't count as breaking any law."

"So, your daughter is a light-hearted person who is not intentionally breaking any law. She just loves fun, so she smiles often and gives names to almost anything. How often have we done these actions ourselves, especially when we're young? We even give people derogatory names when we are angry at them, such as one you would give to a boss.

"Thank you, Ms. Borkowski. You have enlightened us about the character of your daughter." The defence lawyer walked away from her and sat down.

The judge asked, "Does the prosecutor wish to cross-examine this witness?"

There was silence for some seconds. The prosecutor stood up. "Yes, your Honour."

"Ms. Borkowski, your daughter sounds like a very nice young lady but wouldn't you consider some of those actions of which you speak rather immature?"

"Do you think everybody should go through life like a big grump and be serious all the time?"

"When it pertains to the laws, yes. Do you consider her acts to exhibit much maturity?"

"Does maturity mean, being grumpy?"

"I have no more questions, your Honour."

The judge said, "You may step down, Ms. Borkowski."

"Does the defence have any other witnesses?"

"No, your Honour."

"Then, is the prosecutor ready for your summation?"

"Yes, your Honour," responded the prosecutor.

"Is the defence also ready?"

The defence attorney responded, "Yes, your Honour."

"Please proceed," the judge added.

The prosecutor began to speak. "Your Honour, from the defendant's testimony you've heard her admit to all the charges. She has pleaded guilty to naming her slave. Regarding the charge of consorting with a slave, she has admitted to patting its head and almost at the same time smiling at it. These types of activities contravene paragraphs 6.93, 6.97, and 6.101 of the *Slaves Act*. In addition, under section sixty-five of the *Public Order Act*, these very actions are an affront to good public order.

"Now, I know she's trying to excuse her patting and smiling actions or redefine them but the law is clear. These activities, and others, are forbidden, and for good reason. These activities may make a person develop a fondness for a slave, or worse, develop a friendship with it – like a pet, or more. When people do this, it undermines the very foundation of our society. She admitted to knowing the laws but still flouted them. Her mother has supported my argument by implying her daughter acts rather immaturely in her flouting the Law.

"And flout it she did, not just on July twelfth, but, by her admission, for at least six months. As she has had this slave for about a year, for virtually half the time, she broke the law not just once but many times. First, it was the naming, then a progression to more serious acts.

"Her own words have condemned her. Although I admire her truthfulness, she must be found guilty as charged and suffer the punishment necessary for these heinous crimes."

The prosecutor walked over to the table and sat down.

The defence attorney stood up and walked to the centre of the courtroom.

"Your Honour, my client has admitted her error in naming her slave. She apologises for it and is willing to take the penalties associated with her act.

"However, she does not admit to the other two crimes. She has found that praise works better than punishment in any living thing. She deals with children daily in her role as a kindergarten teacher and has had pets in the past. Being a teacher, she has learned positive reinforcement and uses it with her kindergarten students very effectively. She understands the need to tightly control the slaves but her experiences make it an automatic response on her part to place reward above punishment. She feels a light pat on its head wouldn't break the law, especially in a case like this where it was more of an inadvertent act.

"For the third act, being a positive person means she smiles a lot. Frowning and anger are not natural for her, so it's unjust to punish anyone for their nature. She meant no disrespect for the law; she was pleased with the work performed for her that morning and she automatically patted the head of her slave as she would a pet. She was pleased, so she smiled. She smiled for herself, to express her happiness that day. That she did it in front of her slave was unfortunate but she merely expressed how she felt that day.

"In brief, my client has indeed named her slave and she has been honest about it, although she awarded a name that is not normal but a kind of nickname – something you may call a dog or other lower life form, which raises the question of whether it should be considered a name. For her complete cooperation in this case, I ask that any penalty applied be the minimum under the law and the second and third charges be dismissed because there was no intent involved. Her mother confirmed she is a rather happy person who naturally reacts positively to life's experiences."

The defence attorney returned to her table.

The judge sat quietly for about thirty seconds then asked, "Are there any other comments to be made on this case?"

Both attorneys said, "No, your Honour."

She looked at the defendant and asked, "Do you have any words in your defence, before my judgement and sentencing, if that be the case?"

The defendant stood up and said, "Your Honour, I would like to apologise to this court, to my government, friends, neighbours and family, for my transgression in naming my slave. It was disrespectful and shameful of me to do that. I guess I got tired of just saying 'Hey you' or 'slave' all the time but I was wrong.

"The other two acts, although I know they are forbidden, I did inadvertently. I have a particularly good slave and I find it hard not to do what is natural to me and reward it with a pat on the head. My smile was not a form of fondness but of happiness in having good service provided to me. Surely, one can pardon a person who responds automatically to a situation. If I were to smile or laugh at something funny on the holovision and my slave saw me, do it, is that breaking the law? I had no intent to break the law. I beg the court to consider my intent."

The defendant sat down. There was silence for about half a minute.

The judge then spoke, "I recess this session for thirty minutes to allow me time to deliberate on this case."

Everyone in the court stood up. The judge got up and left the courtroom.

In her office, she sat down in her comfortable chair and closed her eyes for several minutes. She then began to dictate her judgment.

After thirty minutes, she entered the courtroom and sat down. The rest of the people followed suit.

The judge set up her viewer showing her dictated notes of judgement, peered down at Jean Borkowski, and said, "Please stand while I read my judgement."

Jean stood up.

"Jean Borkowski, you have pleaded guilty to naming your slave and your plea has been accepted by this court; in other words, I don't think you're insane or you've been coerced into pleading guilty. The matter of the other two charges remains.

"You have offered several excuses for your violation of the law for those. Your first excuse for patting the slave I cannot accept at all. Your second excuse for smiling, I realise, is a strong one. If someone brought you before me on that one charge only, I might have excused it but I must look at all the acts in their entirety. The law is clear and you are not ignorant of the law and its intent. You are a classic case of a violator, as you can see. You named your slave and started down the road to perdition. You graduated from naming it to smiling at it and patting it on the head and back.

I know you feel you have a natural tendency to do it but that cannot be an excuse. Pat your child, pat your dog or cat but do not pat your slave. It's that simple.

"I find you guilty on all counts. Now for your punishment. I have decided not to have you imprisoned; however, I fine you the amount of $50,000, and the police will take your slave from you and destroy it, in case your actions affected it. You will no longer be able to have a slave for the rest of your life. You also will have limited interaction with anyone else's slaves, which means the police will brand you as a violator of the *Slave Act,* so people will be aware of your transgression.

"Note that you got off relatively easily, as the fine could have been higher and you could have been imprisoned for up to fifteen years. You should be thankful to your neighbour for informing us before your situation got worse, or you really could have had much more serious consequences. On behalf of all the population of this planet, we applaud your action in reporting this crime, Ms. McGregor.

"This court is adjourned." She slammed her gavel on the desk.

Everyone stood up, and the judge stood up and left the court.

The defendant sat in her chair for a while, stunned. The full reality hit her but she could not show it, so she fought the urge she felt inside. She had not only condemned herself but she had earned her slave a death sentence. She wanted to cry but had to resist. Two police officers then took her out of the court to complete the necessary documents and later have her branded.

Marie was happy with herself. Everything had gone very efficiently and she had followed due process. She regarded her caseload for the next day and was thankful that no people were on it. When she had finished the review, she headed home with her daughter.

At home, Marie rested for a while. Her slave prepared their supper and for once did not ruin it. After two years, her slave was adjusting to their peculiarities.

After supper, her daughter did her homework while Marie watched a Holovision movie. They both liked to settle in bed relatively early to give them some time to read. Later, she wandered over to her daughter's bed to tuck her in and sat down to talk for a while.

"So, what did you think of the court case this afternoon?" Marie asked.

"I learned a lot about the law. I guess I'll be learning more about it later in school."

"Yes, it's very important to learn about it to avoid being charged with an offence."

"Wow, yes, it's very serious."

"Yes, especially if you want to have your own slave someday. The laws are there for the protection of the individual and society. Governments don't just issue laws for no purpose. We, as citizens, elect our legislators and they formulate the laws but the legislature carries out the will of the people. Their laws are our laws. We want those laws. By voting for our representative, we approve those laws.

"As a society, we must adhere to the laws. Without them, we would have chaos and history has proved over and over what happens when people flout established laws – you have instability, wars, and anarchy. You learned in school and even today in court about some cases of the results of even seemingly mild breaches of the *Slave Act*. First, you name your slave then you smile at and/or pat your slave – which seems harmless but it emboldens the slave, or even if that doesn't happen, it weakens the person to like or even to grow very fond of the slave and that ultimately leads to disaster. Remember the temptation of Eve with the forbidden apple?

"Remember, having a slave is not a right but a privilege. We've had slavery for many years now, because people want to have them to lighten their workload around the home, so the government has put measures in place to allow slavery. However, it comes with many responsibilities, like the slave's proper care and treatment. If people cannot follow the Law concerning slaves, then there is the possibility the government will repeal the Act and this would be a disaster for most people. So, most people would lose this privilege because of the folly of a few. How fair is that to law-abiding people?"

Her daughter nodded her assent, and Marie kissed her on the forehead and left.

A few weeks after the court case, her daughter had a classroom discussion that intrigued her. When she arrived home, as usual, her mother asked, "How was your day at school?"

"Good."

"What did you learn today?"

"We were learning about the great queens of the past and how things were way back then. I love history. Why did we have so many wars back then anyway?"

"There were lots of problems at the time – most people were very poor and were fighting for more territory to feed themselves, or trying to be richer than their neighbours. There was not much of a civilisation back then, more like anarchy and barbarism."

"The royal people sure dressed their slaves oddly."

"Those were the fashions of the times."

"Slaves these days don't have to work as hard now as they seemed to back then."

"Yes, they're a lot better off now. Let me tell you some information that they don't necessarily put in your history books. Most people don't know this, so I'll count on you to discuss only things mentioned in class and not what I'm about to tell you.

"We've always had slaves. During the early years, they had a more significant role. They did a lot of things for us to lighten our load. We even allowed them some decision-making. This allowed us to focus on raising our families during those tough times. In the end, the world became overpopulated and out of control.

"Early on, we did name our slaves. Naming our slaves tended to make them seem more than slaves and some people became emotionally attached to them. How can you properly control a slave that you have an emotional attachment to?

"In time, though, we decided to limit their role as it was becoming problematic. There began to be doubt as to who was running things, so we finally had to reassert ourselves and limit the tasks our slaves could do. The final clarification came with the *Slave Act*, which helped us to control better the relationships between people to their slaves.

"So, the Act made it illegal to name them, talk to them, except to order them to do things or seem to like them by smiling or patting them. We even strictly controlled the numbers of them and the people who can have one. We even weed out the more aggressive ones when they are young. To make sure they will cause no problems, the slaves are eunuchs. There are only a few of them kept for breeding purposes."

"So, we named them!"

"Yes, we generally called them 'men' and gave them individual names at birth according to an old book, the first slave was named Adam.

"It's time to go to sleep now, sweetheart."

"Night, Mom."

Marie tucked her daughter into bed and headed off to her own.

DISILLUSIONED

This is another story from back in the 1960s. I found it in a bundle of handwritten stories in one of my old folders. I typed it into the computer, polished it up and here is a little story of paradise lost.

Once there were people as contented as cows but along came a devil disguised as a snake that showed them the apple tree and tempted them to eat.

Maria was quietly preparing supper for her husband, Fred. They had only married three months ago, and the glow of a bride was still strong.

"Maria," Fred called as he entered the cave.

"Yes?" she answered.

"I brought you something," he said, as he held his hands behind his back.

"Oh, what could it be?" she asked excitedly, "blueberries, grapes . . . or is it something like meat? Maybe chicken, yes?"

"Well, no but you're close," he teased her with a broad grin.

"Come on," she said, as she tried to peek around his back while he twisted himself to keep his gift hidden behind him. He then very reluctantly, as always, gave her the gift. It resided in a little leather bag.

"Umm . . . rabbit, and a peach for dessert," she cried with glee, as she began opening the bag.

"Wait until you see what I've got for you," Fred said.

She peeled back the leather, gazed at two rosy apples inside and said, "This is so beautiful. They must be the first apples of the season."

"I hope they're ripe enough," he responded.

"Oh, they're beautiful. We'll finish supper and eat them for dessert."

"And I see you've cooked a beautiful supper, umm, rabbit. I guess that's the last of the meat for now? I'll get you more meat tomorrow, I promise."

She smiled back at him and they both sat down to eat.

The next morning, he was out hunting when he spotted a hefty boar. He armed his bow and stealthily angled himself downwind to cut down some of the distance between him and the juicy animal. He eased back the cord of the bow gauging the boar's distance then let fly. The arrow caught it right behind the neck. The boar gave out a great squeal of pain and slumped to the ground. Fred edged his way over to the animal but it did not move. He smiled broadly. His father had taught him well. He crouched as he pulled out his cutting stone from the pouch in his quiver and knelt behind his prize to begin preparing it for the short walk home.

Suddenly, some rustling in the bushes startled him. Within seconds after the noise, another man approached him.

"Hi, neighbour, admiring my boar," his neighbour called out.

"What? This is mine. See my arrow sticking from its neck." He looked around the site and spotted another arrow lying about a metre from the boar. "I guess that's your arrow over there," Fred said to the man as he pointed to the other arrow.

The neighbour went over, picked it up and examined it. There was no blood on it. "So, it is. I guess I missed my shot. I guess that will serve as a feast for your young bride, huh?"

Fred watched the other man's frustration at not having any food to bring home for his family. "Do you have enough food to eat?" he asked.

"Hunting has been poor lately. We haven't had meat for some time now. We're doing okay; we've got lots of roots and berries," the neighbour responded.

"Well, neighbour, tonight you and your family shall join us for a feast of our good luck. Just come before the sun sets to make it easy for you to get home in the light. I will cut the boar in half and give you some meat to take home."

The neighbour thanked him and asked him if he needed help to prepare the carcass but Fred turned him down. The neighbour left for home. Fred bled the animal, cleaned out the carcass and headed home.

When he entered his cave with his prize on his back, Maria was ecstatic. Fred told her of his experience with his neighbour while Maria helped him cut up the meat for their neighbours and the evening feast. She then added wood to the fire to get some coals to bake the meat and some roots.

Later in the evening, the neighbour came over with his wife, son, and daughter. They had brought with them some tubers and some fruit to contribute to the meal. The six of them had a pleasant evening of storytelling and singing as they ate their fill. Before the neighbours left, Fred gave them their gift of meat. The mother was so happy she had tears of joy. Their visitors left with much thanks and good cheer.

This was the way it had been for years. Nobody knew differently. In good times, they celebrated, and in bad times they shared their good luck when it came.

The next morning, a solid, glistening object not far from Fred and Maria's cave caught their attention when they got up. It was a cylinder about twenty metres high and ten metres in diameter perched on another cylinder about two metres in diameter and three metres high.

"What is it?" asked Maria in wonder as she and her husband approached the object.

"Don't go any farther. Maybe it's not good," he said to her.

"Everything is good," she retorted.

"I don't know," he answered. "I've never seen anything like this before."

Their neighbours were arriving as they too were curious about the object. While they walked around it, touching its sides, a door opened in the lower cylinder and to everyone's surprise a tall being that looked similar but not identical, to them stepped halfway out. The visitor appeared to be a male and looked even more surprised to see them. Once the shock wore off, the newcomer stepped out of the doorway and another person quickly followed – a female this time.

The foreigners then tried to tell the people they had come from far away to settle on their planet. All the people could make out of it, by signs, was the visitors were going to remain there for a while.

Maria was intently admiring something on the woman's wrist – a watch; but of course, she did not know what it was. The woman noticed this and, to enhance friendly relations, gave it to her. Maria was surprised by the gift but accepted it with great thanks. In response, Maria welcomed the visitors into their home. The foreign woman looked startled. She looked at the cave but was not eager to enter. She preferred to live in their ship even if it was small and cramped.

Realising she and her husband could not live forever in their metal home, and they would have to adopt the ways of the land eventually, she accepted. Her husband was not pleased but showed no unpleasantness on his countenance.

For several days, the visitors remained in the cave. They built an outhouse a distance from the cave and decorated the cave with ornaments. When they finally left to move back into their metal object, the two couples had exchanged customs and practices. Fred and Maria were also learning to speak a new language.

Fred and Maria had a chance to visit the interior of the object and learned about comforts, such as temperature control and artificial food and light, as well as using metal utensils to eat. They noticed their neighbours did not visit them or talk to them much anymore, as the two of them were spending almost all their time with the visitors. Fred had learned to use a new hunting tool that spat out a coloured light to slay his prey. He was not sharing his bounty with his neighbours as he always had, and they resented it.

Maria was quite surprised with the new couple's practices. The woman would often challenge her husband and they did not often share the work.

One day, Maria remarked to Fred about this but he just shrugged his shoulders.

"They seem so advanced, so proper, yet we are so . . . so . . . I don't know," she said.

Daily, she left the cave to visit the newcomers in their home and was mesmerised by all the gadgets they had. This distracted her from household chores, which now was Fred's to do. He ignored her absence though. He wanted things to be the way they were.

"Why don't you get me a hat?" she asked Fred one day.

"A what?" he asked.

"A hat," she answered.

"What's a hat?" he asked.

"Something to put on my head," she replied.

"Where will I find a . . . hat, you call it?"

"Oh, I don't know," she answered. "Maybe I can make one out of bearskin."

"Well, don't ask me for one then. I have enough to do with your leaving the chores undone. Now you want me to hunt a bear?"

So, for the first time in these people's history, there was an argument but it was not happening just here. All over the neighbourhood, their neighbours started squawking. No more did they share; no more was there simple bliss. The next time any men both shot at an animal, they would fight to see who got it.

And that is the way it should be, or should it? They had eaten the apple and no longer would there be peace in paradise.

The visitors intermingled and interbred with the Aboriginals and their progeny spread. As the paint peeled off the majestic shining object pointing toward the sky, a new race was born. A race now brought up in a new way. The great object would remain as a monument to the new life. For generations, it would stand while the NASA lettering flaked away, and the ship would rot and rust into the landscape.

SCARECROW

Here is another story from back in the 1960s. I found it in the same bundle as Disillusioned. I typed it into the computer, polished it up, and here is a little story of love lost.

Francine felt miserable and could feel the churning in her stomach. She was disgusted with everything, even her life.

She was tall, blond-haired, and pretty but had no friends.

She shook the misery out of her for a minute and saw that she was on the outskirts of town. She wanted to think things out. She was deep in thought pitying herself, making herself as miserable as she could to reinforce her thoughts of suicide. She slumped back into her shell.

The sound of a male voice interrupted her thoughts. "Hi, there."

She turned to her left to see a lanky, dark-haired man standing in the middle of a cornfield. He wore dirty rags for clothes and had a dishevelled appearance.

"Hi," she ventured angrily while noting his dress. He had disturbed her thoughts. She stopped walking.

"I hope I didn't disturb you," the man in the field called out. "You looked very serious."

"No, everything's perfectly all right," she said sarcastically.

"What are you angry about?" he asked innocently as he walked closer to the road. He did not like shouting.

"Never mind," she said more softly.

There were a few moments of silence while they looked each other over. He finally took the initiative. "If you don't want to stay . . . I mean, where are you going?"

"Oh, that's none of your business," she said curtly.

"I'm sorry I disturbed you," he said, feeling rebuffed.

She seemed puzzled. This was not the type of person she would normally be talking to. She was more used to city boys; much better dressed and more aggressive.

"Aren't you going to continue on your way?" he asked from the other side of the roadside ditch.

"I don't know. I'm not going anywhere in particular," she responded more amicably.

"Something's the matter?" he asked.

"Yes."

"I guess many people have problems these days," he continued.

"Too many," she said sadly.

He crossed the ditch and said, "I shouldn't do this but I guess it doesn't matter."

It did. As soon as he stepped off the cornfield some waiting crows sitting on the power lines headed towards the patch. He re-entered the field and started chasing them away.

"I'll come and help you," she called out as she hurried into the field and ran after some of the crows. It took a while to shoo the birds back onto their roosts.

After they had dislodged the crows from their meals, she said, "Gee that was fun. I enjoyed that. I'll stay here to help you. Even though it looks boring, we can leave the field, let the birds return, and run after them for some fun. Is this what you do? I mean cultivate this corn?"

"I don't cultivate it. I keep the crows away," he corrected her.

"Huh?"

"I'm a scarecrow," he responded.

"This is what you do all day; chase crows when they enter the field?"

"Sure, the straw scarecrows don't fool the crows anymore. They ignored them, so the farmers turned to real scarecrows to keep the birds under control. Now the crows know we're serious."

"I've seen all kinds of guys with all kinds of interesting jobs. They bored me to death. Men are all the same." She sighed. ". . . Oh, sorry." She stopped her line of conversation, a little ashamed.

"That's all right. What's your name?"

"Francine but just call me Frances if you don't mind."

"Frances, that's a nice name."

"I don't mind it but I hate Francine. What's yours?"

"Steve but everyone just calls me Scary."

She smiled, "That's funny. You don't mind being called that?"

"No, that's what I do."

"You know, I've forgotten about my problems. I like the peace out here. I've lived in the city all my life and I've never left it. It's noisy and dirty and the people are not that friendly – especially the men."

"Really?"

"I don't know why but it's true." She liked this boy and his simple nature. It was refreshing in comparison to the city boys.

"You look better now," he smiled.

"I feel better," she replied with a more cheerful tone.

"Good."

She was becoming attracted to Scary. There was silence for a long while.

"Sit down," he suggested.

"Will the crows come back?"

"We can sit on the fence, that'll make it less likely."

She found it uncomfortable sitting on the thin edge of the fence but did not give it a second thought. The fence only spanned a short distance along this part of the field. It had originally encompassed the entire field but over the last ten years or so it had fallen into disrepair.

"You know, I had planned to commit suicide. I've grown to hate men but . . . it doesn't matter now."

"Why?"

"Because I've had many bad experiences with them. To me, they're just a bunch of animals."

"That doesn't sound good."

"It isn't."

They sat on the fence for over two hours getting to know each other. She looked at her watch when she noticed the sun had dipped low in the sky. "Oh, gosh, it's getting late. I'd better go," she said.

They looked into each other's eyes for a few minutes more, then she hopped off the fence and they exchanged goodbyes.

The walk back to town seemed so short. She kept thinking of the time she had spent with Scary. She arrived back at her apartment. Instead of eating and going out again, she decided to stay home. Tonight, she wanted a quiet night.

In the morning, she got up early. She had to get away again and see Scary. She knew the people she worked for would be angry with her. She was not sure what she would do when she got back again but she did not care. She would worry about that later. Right now, she wanted to be with Scary, helping him to guard the field from the crows.

She retraced her steps from the day before, all the while thinking Scary would not be there. Maybe it had been a dream and he a piece of her imagination but she was wrong. She spotted him in the field. She smiled and ran toward him. When he spotted her, he raced to her too and they embraced.

They spent the entire day together. He shared his meal and water with her. She pressed him for their first kiss. She was in love. For a long time, they lay in the field looking at the clouds in the sky.

She started to wonder what she would do with him. How about her work in the city? If she went back now, how would she explain herself to her manager? He would not be very sympathetic; in fact, he would be furious.

"It's getting late," she suddenly said. "I'm afraid to go back. I have a job and my manager is not going to be very happy I'm missing time from work. I'd like to stay with you."

"I don't know what my parents would say. I'd like to stay with you, too. It gets lonely out here with just the crows."

"Do you think your parents would mind if I worked out here too?"

"They're relatively poor; I don't know if they'd like to feed or pay for another scarecrow."

"You can't make very much at this job."

"I don't make anything."

"What?" she asked in surprise. "Your father is the owner, isn't he?"

"Yes but . . . I'm sort of a . . ."

"A what?"

"A slave."

"There are no slaves anymore, except . . . no, you're not . . . you can't be."

"Yes."

"A machine?" she said incredulously.

"Yes."

"How can you be a machine? You eat sandwiches and drink water! You even kiss!"

"I'm made to be as human-like as possible. I'm built with a digestive tract and everything. I look like a man and feel like a man. I'm a fully functional male, and yes, I can kiss, and more. I didn't even know I was a machine until a few years ago when my father told me he adopted me as a son. They built me to be a young man, so my makers even put memories in my brain about my life as a baby and a child growing up; a full history. I'm his son."

"No, no, no . . . You're a machine." She stood up quickly, screaming, and ran down the road. Men did not accept her, now this finished her. She had fallen in love with a machine, a perfect image of a man.

The thought of suicide re-entered her mind. She sickened. She could not love a machine. She wanted to get away from men and live a normal life but that always seemed impossible.

Frances re-entered the city she had left, took the elevator to the top floor of a tall building, and found her way to a window. She opened it. Something was trying to stop her from her fate and she hesitated. Her mind fought. She could not do this; it was not right. Slowly, hesitatingly she slid herself to the ledge with her face toward the wall. She could not look down. She was in near hysteria as she grew increasingly feverish. If only she could stay on the ledge a little longer. Something burned from inside her. She suddenly went limp, and fell backwards, careening off the side of the ledge to her doom.

All the king's horses and all the king's men could never put Frances together again as she smashed into thousands of pieces of circuits, wires, and gears.

THE FLOOD

This is one of the shortest stories I wrote in the 1960s. A television commercial that ran frequently at that time was its inspiration.

He grasped for his next hold. He was so exhausted that he finally had to rest. He felt that he could not continue any longer. He shook with the effort that he had made to get as far as he had. He looked up. It seemed that he had much farther to go. He almost shuddered at the thought. He could not turn back now; he had come too far. It would be a descent to humiliation, or possibly a slip to his death. No, the only way now was up, up into the unknown.

Above him was light, a dim light that shone in an equal period of lengths which came from an unmoving source and was cool, orange, and distant.

Here, years and months had no meaning. They called their world "Solace" after their God of Light, for they feared the light which often brought them terrible floods and death but also nourishment, renewal, and growth. It brought a life of two extremes, of boom or bust, of all or nothing.

Life made them tough. Life was too short for sleep; just eat, work, and survive. Children would be born, age, and die. There was no sleep or rest. The people accepted the floods, for it was part of their life.

He looked down. He had quite a lead on his compatriots, those brave souls struggling their way up behind him. They were having an even harder time than he was. Many would not make it to the top. Several had already backed out earlier in the climb. Some had slipped and fallen into oblivion but all had committed. He knew they were counting on him. If he led, they would follow.

It was hard to say whether the climb was getting easier. The climb was vertical but as one got higher, it got drier. Whereas the earlier part of the trek was wet and slippery, now the way was so dry that solid handholds were hard to find as pieces tumbled off the cliff face with their weight. Dehydration was now another problem. He was beginning to feel its effects. He knew that he should not tarry; to stall meant time lost, and time lost meant certain death.

His resolve faltered. He tried to peer farther down past his friends but all he could see now was black; black deeper than a starless night. He knew that below him, in the blackness, was home.

Overcrowded with billions upon billions of his compatriots, his world was built on the graves of those before. All there was for water was the well that had become polluted and hardly fit to drink. There was pestilence and strife now. Death was in the land. Famine had come to visit. The starving masses had become unruly and were resorting to cannibalism to stay alive.

Now, their population clamoured for action. Someone had to do something. The revolution was in the air. Someone had to volunteer to scout out new land, a home with food and fresh water. If they did not make the trip soon the floods would begin. Without notice, the skies would let out with a torrent that would wash many of them away. They knew not from where and did not care. Life was too short, too cruel.

His mind pulled back into focus. He started up once more and quickened his pace up the cliff. He could hear his friends behind him. He paused and allowed them to almost catch up.

He had volunteered to make this journey. At the time it had seemed necessary but now he was not sure. The distance from the home he loved was weakening his resolve. He reached out and pulled himself up once again. No one in living memory had made this journey and returned to tell of it.

The climb was much slower now but he had to do it. He had to be an example to those below who were struggling with him. He kept crawling forward. The light was becoming more intense now, the way clearer. He stopped again to rest. He was almost delirious now. He looked up again. Yes, it was close now, one more run at it. The thought revived his sagging resolve. He was running on pure will. Again, his companions had almost caught up. He gripped the side and pulled, then another hand-hold and pull. Finally, he was at the top. All motion below him stopped. He looked down and could sense all their attention on him. He could now describe the new land he saw and his compatriots could pass the message down the line.

He looked around. "I see light, lots of light," he shouted to those below but he was disappointed. It was a desert drier and more barren than anyone knew. He looked more closely to see if he could find someplace, they could live. He tried to put into words what he saw.

Suddenly, a shadow moved over the light and giant boulders tumbled down from the sky. One just missed him but others knocked some of his compatriots off their perches and into the blackness below. In time, he could hear the terrified screams of the population far below them.

He became terrified himself. The horror of what he heard sent chills through his body. Before he could decide what to do, a torrent of water swept over him. He hung on but there was no firm hand-hold. The flood had begun. He tried desperately to hold his position. He could see and hear his compatriots tumble into the black horror below and see the sparkle of a foam-like material bubble up from the black.

Yes, it was the flood but this flood brought a death more terrifying than they had ever known. He could hold on no longer.

* * *

In a bathroom, a woman hummed as she worked. In her hands, she carried a little can. She stopped humming, popped the lid tightly on it, looked at it, and smiled as she reached to place it back in the cupboard while saying quietly to herself "Once in every week Drano in every drain."

ABOUT THE AUTHOR

Michael has had the urge to write since before his teen years, but has not had much time to spend doing it. Now that he is retired, he is able to fulfil his life-long ambition and has pulled out some story ideas of his youth and mixed them with inspiration from the present to write stories and novels. He is an avid reader, particularly of history and science fiction. His favourite TV shows (besides the cowboys) from his youth were Twilight Zone, Outer Limits and Star Trek. His favourite authors are Lester Del Rey, Rod Serling, Isaac Asimov, Robert Heinlein, Arthur C. Clark and Ray Bradbury. He lives in Canada.